MURDER AT WINDMILL LAKE

JUDY KEIGHTLEY

COZY HOUSE PRESS

COZY HOUSE PRESS
MAKE A DATE WITH MURDER

An Imprint for GracePoint Publishing (www.GracePointPublishing.com)

GracePoint Matrix, LLC
624 S. Cascade Ave
Suite 201
Colorado Springs, CO 80903
www.GracePointMatrix.com
Email: Admin@GracePointMatrix.com
SAN # 991-6032

ISBN-13: (Paperback) –978-1-951694-62-3

eISBN: (eBook) - 978-1-951694-61-6

Books may be purchased for educational, business, or sales promotional use.
For bulk order requests and price schedule contact:
Orders@GracePointPublishing.com

I would like to dedicate this book to my lovely cousin Kate and her family who live and work in Holland and who were the inspiration for this novel.

THE HISTORY OF THE FOLMAR WINDMILL

The windmill is a replica of a windmill in Holland where Frank de Jong's grandfather was the master miller before its destruction during World War ll. The mill was called Arend, Dutch for Eagle, and located in Harlingen in the Netherlands.

Frank de Jong was an engineer, instrument maker, and created sketches and blueprints before making a wooden model of the windmill after a visit to Holland in the early 1970s. For years he worked constantly on the project sometimes alone, and sometimes with other men including his brother Eike.

It took one summer to build the mill's cement foundation consisting of a total of sixty-seven feet above ground concrete pillars using over 1000 bags of cement. Each pillar weighs more than a ton and is buried about one metre below the ground.

The mills tower and the adjacent building are made of wood and took approximately two years each to construct. Long, straight trees went into the mill, sourced from de Jong's own woodland and purchased from his neighbours.

From the ground to the top of the sails the windmill is ninety-five feet tall. It stands on a three acre island surrounded by a beautiful spring-fed forty acre lake. If you look directly upwards you can see the cap of the windmill with the name Folmar inscribed on a piece of wood cut to resemble the horns and head of a mountain goat. Frank believed this gave the windmill strength and he shared this incredible building with visitors until the time of his death in 1999.

The property was purchased in 2013 and is now open to visitors again through the establishment of Windmill Lake and Eco Park. Although the windmill will not be open for tours, entry to the park is free and the new owners welcome visitors to come, learn, and enjoy the beautiful legacy that Frank created in Huron County.

JAN VERMEER (1632-1675)

Jan Vermeer was a Dutch painter whose ability to utilize varied tones of colour in order to convey the unique texture and appearance of objects, is quite probably un-surpassed in the history of painting. Known also as Jan van der Meer van Delft, the artist was born in 1632 in Delft, Holland. His father was an art dealer and innkeeper. It is not known who Vermeer's teachers were, but his works show the influence of the School of Utrecht and of Carel Fabritius who died in Delft in 1654. He was received as Master of the Guild of St. Luke in 1653 and served four times on its board of governors. By his marriage to Catherine Bolens in 1653, he had eleven children. When he died at the age of forty-three, eight of them were still minors. Vermeer was buried in Delft on December 15, 1675.

Living in modest circumstances, Vermeer occasionally was forced to borrow money. To add to his income he tried, not too successfully, to deal in art. A slow, painstaking worker, he produced only a small number of pictures, most of which sold after his death. Of twenty-one mentioned and described in an auction sale in May 16, 1696, sixteen can still be identified.

Despite the eager efforts of modern collectors and dealers to find unknown Vermeers, efforts of which have been rewarded by the appearance of several clever forgeries, the list of genuine pictures by Vermeer, is still small, thirty-nine or forty at best.

ONE

Tom stood by the water's edge looking out across the glistening lake. It seemed incredible to think that someone had created the man-made lake and then constructed the majestic windmill which was now perched proudly upon a wooden platform near the side of the lake. *Who had been the previous owner*, Tom thought as he watched a gangly heron swoop and skim across the water in one fluid movement, long beak in and out and then back in the air again, fish in its mouth.

There were a few paddle boarders out on the lake, but most of the activity was centered upon wakeboarding. Indeed, it had been Abby and Ella, his granddaughters' idea to spend the afternoon at the eco-park. The previous summer they had attended a wakeboard and art camp and had loved every minute of it. When Tom and Rose's daughter, Jessica, had asked if Abby and Ella could spend a couple of weeks with them, Rose had immediately registered the girls for an afternoon at Windmill Lake. Judging by the squeals of delight he could hear they were having a great time although it would soon be time to head back home.

Tom looked at his watch and then turned towards the windmill. It was then that he remembered the original owner's name, Frank de Jong. He had read about the amazing project which had taken almost twenty years to complete and had finally opened in 1989. Apparently, Frank de Jong had modelled the design of the windmill based on a mill that was located in Harlingen in Holland. His grandfather had worked as the master miller at this mill. It had taken the whole of one summer just to build the foundations and erect the concrete pillars which would support the whole structure. The actual windmill itself would end up being over ninety-five feet tall and was built from trees grown on the de Jong's own property woodland.

Walking towards where Rose was sitting watching the girls wakeboard, Tom almost bumped into a man who appeared to be in a tremendous hurry. He was carrying a black, tubular fishing rod case and was wearing, rather incongruously for the time of year, a full-length Barber jacket.

"Oh, I'm sorry," Tom said amicably. "I didn't see you."

"*Potverdore*," the man hissed as he pushed past Tom and continued walking briskly towards the car park.

What a rude man, Tom thought as he watched him in the distance get in a car and begin to drive away. *Oh, well, it takes all sorts*, he mused. Tom was about to join Rose when he stopped suddenly and looked back towards the windmill. What was it that had caught his attention back there? He retraced his steps to where the windmill sat on its concrete pillars. Looking up and around Tom scanned the area with his sharp eyes. It was then that he saw a pair of legs partially concealed from view protruding from beneath the platform.

With some trepidation, Tom walked over to the structure and peered underneath the deck. What he saw was not a pretty sight. A man lay sprawled on the ground with what looked like half his head blown off. Blood and particles of brain matter were splattered everywhere. Tom felt his stomach lurch and before he could prevent himself, he had vomited violently into the grass. Wiping his mouth with the back of his hand, he groped in his pocket for his phone and punched in 911.

TWO

DCI John Hargreaves looked at his watch and calculated that it would take him one and a quarter hours to reach Bayfield. Just to confirm his reckoning, he had checked on map-quest and sure enough it estimated that it would take one hour and twenty minutes. *Near enough*, he thought.

London Serious Crimes Unit had received the phone call from Goderich Dispatch at 3:30 p.m. and he had been on the road within half an hour of that call. He was to drive to Windmill Lake Eco Park, which sounded fascinating.

What was an Eco Park, John thought as he drove out of London towards Arva and Lucan, and *for that matter, what was wakeboarding?*

It was a beautiful day and the countryside looked positively bucolic with the vast fields of corn and horse farms dotted by the side of the road.

If he had been driving back in the U.K. he would almost certainly have been in traffic jams, bumper to bumper, overhead cameras recording every move. This felt like a time warp to him, a trip down memory lane to the days of his youth when one could drive in the countryside and not be jostling neck to neck with other cars. John drove through the town of Exeter smiling at the familiarity of names from the old country. He had, himself, lived at one time of his life in a small village not far from Exeter in Dorset, all of which seemed strangely remote to him now.

He reached Brucefield and pulled over to look at his GPS. It appeared that there were two different ways to reach the Eco-Park, one straight on towards the town of Clinton, the other went through the village of Bayfield. He decided to turn left and take the route through Bayfield. As he passed a shop called Millingtons on the corner of Mill Street and the highway, he looked at the sign that said Antiques and Chinese Crafts. His wife Mary would have begged him to stop if she had been there with him. John sighed deeply and continued to drive over a railway line and on through another small village called Varna and finally to Bayfield. In the distance, at the end of Cameron Street, he could see the sparkling water of Lake Huron. This he would have to explore, but not now, he had a murder to investigate and an eco-park to find.

His GPS took him right on Highway 21, across the Bayfield River and up to Bayfield River Road. There was what looked like a motel called The Ashwood on the corner with a restaurant and patio attached. Maybe he would be able to grab a spot of dinner there afterwards, John mused feeling already rather hungry, as he had missed having lunch. Bayfield River Road wound its way past a trailer park called The Old Homestead on the left-hand side and a modern estate of houses called Carriage Lane on the right. Then he drove past what looked like hop-poles and saw a sign that said, Bayfield Brewery.

This definitely was a place he earmarked to visit at some later date, and then he was there looking down and across at a windmill and a splendid lake and a small sign that said, Windmill Lake Eco Park.

THREE

He pulled into the car park alongside three OPP police cruisers. John walked across to what looked almost like an island, where a large man-made channel ran to his left at the top of which was the wakeboarding winch and mechanism to drag a wakeboarder across the water. *It looked a bit like water skiing,* he thought, pausing to watch as a young woman valiantly tried to keep herself standing whilst taking hold of the handle before falling into the water.

John could see a cluster of people in the distance standing at the foot of a windmill which appeared to be wrapped around with yellow plastic police tape now fluttering about in the late afternoon breeze. An attractive young woman dressed only in a bathing suit walked up to him and held out her hand.

"I'm the owner of the Eco Park, although my father owns the windmill and all the rest of the property. This is a terrible thing to have happened."

John took her hand and looked at her earnest face saying, "We'll get it sorted, don't you worry and, if it's any consolation, in my experience, terrible though this may be, you will most certainly get a lot of press out of it, which can't be too bad for your business."

The young woman looked shocked and was about to make some snappy retort when she was interrupted by a tall man who introduced himself as Sergeant Flowers.

"DCI Hargreaves," John said extending his hand to the Sergeant, "My first body since joining the Serious Crimes Unit, but not by any means my first murder case. You're looking at a seasoned cop here, my lad."

Sergeant Flowers didn't quite know what to say, in fact he had been initially shocked by the appearance of the six-foot two black man dressed smartly in a grey suit complete with a shirt and tie, and when he spoke, he sounded totally and utterly English with a plumy voice reminiscent of some old British movies he had watched as a kid.

"If you'd like to come this way, sir, I'll show you the body." He led the way to the windmill and the group of people standing in a huddle around it.

A young woman wearing rimless glasses dressed in casual jeans and a black t-shirt stepped forward and introduced herself. Peering intensely at John she held out her hand saying, "I'm Constable Holly Ryan, your IT girl. Any computer work you need doing, well, I'm the one to go to."

Two more young men approached John introducing themselves respectively as Constables Elliot and Brown. His predecessor, DCI Parker had obviously formed a good, united team whom all looked keen and ready to work at short notice, but also looked young enough to be his children.

Sergeant Flowers pointed to where a pair of legs protruded from underneath the windmill's platform. He handed a pair of blue latex gloves to DCI Hargreaves and pointed to the planks of wood already laid down forming a pathway to the body.

"The SOC team have already been and gone, sir, but we thought that it would be prudent to preserve the area until the body has been removed. We are still waiting for Dr. Green, our local forensics officer, but he's tied up in court right now and said that he'd get here as soon as he could."

DCI Hargreaves bent down to take a closer look at the body. As he took in the blown off scalp his stomach lurched, he managed to hold the bile from rising up to his throat but did observe vomit close to where he was standing.

"Which one of you puked up your lunch here," he asked pointing to the vomit on the grass.

"None of us did, sir, but I believe our key witness, the man who actually found our victim, he's standing over by the lake, well, the poor man couldn't help throwing up. It's not a pretty sight, sir."

"Do you know who he is?" DCI Hargreaves asked.

"You mean the dead man or our witness, sir?" Sergeant Flowers asked with a bit of a twinkle in his eye and a twitch of a smile on his face.

"The witness, you daft bugger, although it would be great if we knew who our John Doe was too!"

The Sergeant laughed as he answered, "The man over there is called Tom Blair. His wife and he are well known in the community. They were great friends of Susan, umm. I mean DCI Parker. I'll introduce you to him if you'd like, sir."

John nodded and followed the Sergeant over to where a man in his late fifties with greying hair and a rugged face, looked deep in thought gazing across the sparkling lake. He fairly jumped when Sergeant Flowers called out his name and introduced him to DCI Hargreaves.

FOUR

Tom was quite taken aback at the sight of the huge, suited, handsome man. His immediate thoughts were that he looked just like the television character called Luther. Idris Elba, he thought was the name of the actor who played the part of Luther. He would have to ask Rose. *My, my,* Tom thought, *who would have thought that DCI Susan Parker would have been replaced by this Luther-like detective, it certainly was a turn up for the books,* and once again he couldn't wait to tell Rose.

"Good afternoon, sir," DCI Hargreaves said politely shaking hands with Tom. "I understand that you discovered the body."

"Yes, I saw the pair of legs protruding from underneath the windmill and when I got closer, I found that poor man with half his head blown off. It really turned my stomach." Tom said, pulling a face at the recollection.

"Did you see anything else at all suspicious?"

Tom was quiet as he thought back and then he answered the inspector, "Yes, actually there was a man I bumped into just minutes before I discovered the body. He was in a big hurry and almost knocked me over."

"Could you describe this man?"

"Well, he was wearing an oil skinned jacket like a barber and was carrying a fishing rod case. He muttered something as we collided, and it sounded foreign to me."

"What sort of age was the man?"

DCI Hargreaves was writing everything down in a small notebook.

Tom answered, "I would say he was probably in his late forties or early fifties. He looked a bit worn, if you know what I mean. Thin, brown shoulder length hair, and a pale complexion. That's about all I can remember. Now, can I go detective, as my wife and grandchildren I'm sure will be anxiously waiting my return."

"Thank you, Tom, you have been most helpful. We'll have to get a full statement from you later, but for now you can go home."

Tom thought to himself that the new DCI was a very polite and a pleasant enough fellow although he was not one single bit like DCI Parker. With a pang of sadness thinking about Susan Parker, Tom drove off ready to give Rose all the news.

FIVE

He had already checked into The Albion a couple of days ago and had decided to stay on a few extra days. There was one thing that time had taught him and that was not to do anything in a rush. If he was to suddenly check out of the hotel alarm bells might go off with the establishment, particularly as he had originally booked for five nights. No, he would stay put and plan what to do next. But first he needed to check out his prize, what he had dreamt about every single day for the past twenty years.

Grabbing hold of the fishing rod case he gently pried the lid open and put his hand inside. Rolled up was a thick canvas. Karel slowly pulled the canvas out and tentatively unrolled it. There, before him in all its glory, was the painting, *The Milkmaid*, possibly one of Johannes Vermeer van Delft's greatest masterpieces, and still as beautiful as the last time that he had studied it over twenty years ago.

That was another lifetime when Gerrit and he were at the peak of their profession and living the high life, rubbing shoulders with fellow art critics and attending many art exhibitions at the Rijks Museum in Amsterdam. Gerrit had been the knowledgeable one of the two of them; he had in fact had a background in fine art specialising in the great artists of the Dutch Golden Ages, in particular the work of Vermeer.

Indeed, it had been his passion as an art restorer that had led them down the path of art forgery and finally, theft. It had been so easy and simple at the time, Gerrit would be commissioned to clean a painting and often the Rijks Museum would employ his services. They had a brilliant painter, Gert, who could copy anything so realistically that no one would ever know the difference between the copy and the original. Part of his success was that he painted the reproductions using the same arcane methods of the seventeenth century artists.

He heated and roasted clay, oxidised lead in vinegar, and ground pigments from stone and ore. He roasted cobalt, melted quartz and potash, creating vermillion, madder, carmine weld, azurite and smelt, all the colours used by the great Dutch Masters. It was painstaking work, but the results were magnificent.

Somehow using the ancient ground powders plus the one added speciality of Vermeer, lapis lazuli, seemed to bring out the luminosity and intensity that modern day paints seemed to lack, and there lay his success. The ability to make his own paints parallel to the old master's, was indeed one of his greatest skills, one which Gerrit and Karel put to good use.

Gert, the artist employed by Van Heuzen Restoration, was commissioned to paint at least one forgery each month, replacing the originals with his reproductions. Their downfall came ultimately with trying to sell the artwork. It was one thing forging great masters, but quite another selling the paintings on at auction houses which all required categorically documented authenticity of the painting.

What they learnt early on was that even the so-called scholars of art history sometimes found it difficult to spot a forgery when traditional paints had been used. Soon a small fortune had been amassed after Karel and Gerrit finally found a market for the real paintings in obscure countries like Kazakhstan, Columbia, several of the islands in the Caribbean, and, of course, the United States.

SIX

The last Vermeer to be reproduced prior to the real one being transported to the United States, had led them to disaster. Karel and Gerrit had met an interesting man at one of the art exhibitions they had attended in Amsterdam. His name was Folkert de Jong and he was over visiting his relatives in Holland. The men had struck up a conversation and soon had learnt all about the windmill Folkert had built in a small village called Bayfield in Ontario, Canada. The man was passionate about his project and by the end of the evening he had invited the two men to visit him in Canada. This provided the perfect excuse to bring *The Milkmaid*, to its new owner, a rich philanthropist from Michigan. They would bring the painting to Canada and make arrangements for the buyer to collect it from them in Bayfield. Visiting the De Jong's was a perfect plan, but like all best laid plans it did not go accordingly.

The two men, Karel and Gerrit, had arrived at Pearson International Airport in Toronto and rented a car, their precious cargo stored in a fishing rod case. They got to the de

Jong's Windmill with no hitches and then telephoned the American buyer. That was when Karel began to smell a rat. The American kept asking questions about the provenance of the painting and it just had not felt right.

After much discussion, they had decided to hide the Vermeer in its fishing rod case underneath the windmill, tucked securely behind the rafters of the platform holding up the structure. Their plan was to return later to retrieve it when they were certain that they were not being set up by the American.

As it transpired, the two of them had been met at Pearson Airport by undercover officers and had been escorted back to Holland, where they had been imprisoned for twenty years for grand theft and forgery. Karel and Gerrit had been released on parole after serving seventeen years. They could not leave the country for two further years. In the interim, the windmill and sixty-five acres of land had changed hands a couple of times, but, fortunately, the windmill itself had remained untouched, although largely unloved, until the new owners had ideas of totally renovating the mill.

Karel and Gerrit had prayed that the fishing-rod case had been hidden well enough under the platform to escape any detection, but it was imperative to retrieve it as quickly as possible.

As soon as their parole was up, the two of them had booked flights to Canada that July and, on arriving, had immediately rented a car and driven to Bayfield. Arriving at the windmill they were astounded to find Wakeboarding and Eco Park set up and people, mostly young kids, having fun on the manmade lake. The windmill, however, stood a little away from the crowds of people.

The two men had made a beeline for it and had almost

reached their destination when an attractive young woman approached them introducing herself as the owner and saying,

"Can I help you two?" she had asked in a friendly, but assertive manner.

Karel had spoken first, as his English was much better than his partner, Gerrit.

"Ya, we were wishing to see the windmill. We come from Holland and had heard about the man who built the windmill in honour of his grandfather." Karel had smiled his most beguiling smile and put out his hand.

"By the way, I'm Karel and this is my friend Gerrit."

"Sure, you can have a quick look at the windmill, but normally this is only for wake and paddle boarders. I must go now, enjoy looking, but please do not touch anything. My father is painstakingly restoring the windmill to its past glory and he wouldn't take kindly to any interference."

The men had nodded and waited until she had turned her back before walking quickly towards the windmill. Twenty years ago, they had hidden the fishing rod case directly above the fourth concrete pillar underneath the wooden platform which supported the whole structure. Now, looking up at the wooden planks straddling the concrete pillars it had been hard to see anything.

"Gerrit, hold your phone up here, we need some light."

Gerrit turned on his flashlight app on his cellphone and held it up high. It had cast long shadows, but soon they could see the cylindrical case wedged carefully between the pillar and platform. Karel had quickly pulled the case down with his back to Gerrit, he had opened the container, and with one quick movement, he had turned. His right hand appeared to be holding a small handgun with a silencer attached. Before

Gerrit could utter a single word, the muffled explosion quieted his voice forever.

As Karel stepped over his partner's legs, he had muttered, "Ik heb je niet meer nodig." *I don't need you anymore. Farewell my friend.*

He had just walked a few metres from the windmill when an older man wearing khaki shorts and a red t-shirt bumped straight into him and they had made eye contact for a brief second as Karel swore loudly, "Potverdore!" and pushed rudely past the man, making a hurried exit toward the car park. Now, here he was sitting in his bedroom at The Albion looking at the priceless Vermeer and wondering what his next move should be.

SEVEN

Rose had taken Abby and Ella home shortly after Tom had beckoned her over and told her quietly about the body found under the windmill. The girls remained ignorant of the murder and, although reluctant to leave their wakeboarding, had soon settled in front of the television with a plate of homemade cookies and milk. Rose busied herself in the kitchen making a spaghetti pie for supper while at the same time dwelling on the murder. She could hardly wait for Tom to come home and fill her in with all the details. One hour later, with the pie almost ready and two hungry girls waiting for their dinner, Tom finally arrived back home. *He looks thoroughly exhausted*, Rose thought as she put the kettle on for a cup of tea.

"Rose, you never will guess who has replaced Susan as DCI at the Serious Crimes Unit. Can you remember that British police show that we both watched last year called *Luther?* Well, the new DCI is a complete look-a-like. He speaks with quite a plumb English accent, but seems very down to earth. We should invite him over for dinner sometime."

She hadn't seen Tom quite so animated in quite awhile. The new DCI must have made a big impression. The kettle boiled and she made the tea, not wanting to enquire about the murder in front of Abby and Ella even though she was absolutely itching to hear the details. Instead she asked Tom no further questions and got on with serving up their dinner. After they had cleared everything away and settled the girls down, Rose decided to take their dogs, Puff and Ben, for a quick walk. She looked at her watch and thought that maybe her sister Kate might be home, although it was only six thirty and she generally didn't get back before seven. Volunteering at the animal rescue centre in Goderich plus working three days a week at the library had kept her sister from brooding too much over the state of her affairs. When her ex had gone off with her best friend Natalie, Kate's whole world had seemingly come tumbling down. It had taken a drastic move across the country from Kelowna in B.C. to Bayfield, to heal the festering wound and now, Rose thought, it had paid off. Kate looked the happiest she had been in years. Her skin glowed, she had lost some weight, but biggest of all, she was smiling and laughing again.

Puff and Ben tugged at their leashes almost dragging Rose over in their eagerness to reach Kate's cottage, situated near the end of Louisa Street. It was a charming, surprisingly spacious house although from the outside it looked tiny. It had two bedrooms and an open plan living room and kitchen with a separate laundry and bathroom. The house was set back from the road and was almost hidden by a cedar hedge planted in the front. Kate had fallen in love at first sight and within six weeks, had moved in. It amazed Rose just how quickly her sister had adjusted to village life. She had joined the Bridge Club and played Mahjong in between helping at the animal rescue in Goderich. The only thing missing in her life was a man and this was something that Kate was in no hurry to find. Rose had suggested that she go online dating or maybe she could try speed-dating. There just had to be someone out there because, who wouldn't fall for her big hearted, lovely sister, Rose thought.

There was no sign of Kate's beat up old Subaru, but just as Rose and the dogs were about to walk home, Kate pulled into the drive.

"Hi, there, Sis" she boomed out loudly, "Watcha doing here?"

"Oh, I just came by for a chat. I've got some news. Can I come in?"

"Sure, I'll open a bottle of Chardonnay. Give me a minute to wash my hands. I've been mucking out the kennels."

Rose pulled a face but smiled to herself. Ben and Puff sniffed the air and followed Kate into the bathroom, smelling her legs and shoes intently.

"They can smell the dogs from the rescue. Oh, but Rose, I almost brought one of them home with me, a tiny fox terrier called Lucy. She's adorable."

"Well, why didn't you then? You've got plenty of room for a dog here."

"I'm going to think about it, Rose. She certainly has got my heart beating faster. You should see how she sits up and paws the air when she wants to get your attention, she's adorable."

Kate moved into the kitchen and opened the fridge, "Ah, yes, I knew that there was an opened bottle here," she grabbed two wine glasses and poured them both a generous helping. "Let's go and sit out on the patio, shall we?"

They pushed the glass sliding doors from the living room onto the patio. Two bright red Muskoka chairs sat solidly on the paved area. The two sisters sat down, and Rose proposed a toast, "To the new DCI John Hargreaves."

"You mean to tell me that Susan's been replaced by a man? Come on, Rose, tell all."

By the time Rose had finished telling Kate what little she knew about the new DCI, her sister's ears had started to prick.

"So, there was a murder at Windmill Lake? What's wrong with the place, Rose, so many murders. Bayfield must be considered the murder capital of Ontario!" They both laughed although there was some truth in Kate's thinking.

Rose and Tom had been involved in one way or another with at least six murders in as many years.

"You know something, Kate, I really, really miss my friend Susan Parker because she always kept me abreast of the investigations."

"Well, you know what you have to do, big sis, that's to invite this hunky Luther look-a-like around for dinner. Oh, and be sure to invite me too!"

"Funny you should suggest that, Tom said the same thing. I suppose I could pop around to The Lion's Hall where I presume, they'll be holding the enquiry. Yes, I'll do that tomorrow. Now, what was your day like?"

An hour later Rose returned home to find Tom playing Scrabble with the girls. She still hadn't asked him about the murder.

EIGHT

J ohn looked around the room at his team, all four of them, and then he looked at the actual space at his disposal, courtesy of The Lion's Club of Bayfield. There was an old-fashioned chalk board spanning the whole width of the room, and a free-standing white board had been placed by the side of a large conference table. At the other end of the room opposite the chalk board, was what looked like a kitchen, a sink, microwave oven, fridge, and cabinets beneath a work counter.

This was all a far cry from the Serious Crimes Unit in London or, indeed, back in England in Bristol where he had lived and worked for over twenty years. In both those offices there was always a buzz of activity with phones ringing constantly and people tapping away at their computers. Here the only sign of a computer was one parked in front of the sole female in the room although he had noticed a stack of iPads sitting on the end table and John wondered what they were there for.

As if reading his mind Sergeant Flowers put up his hand to

speak. "Sir, DCI Parker made us all communicate on these iPads. Do you want us to do the same?"

John looked aghast, "No way, man. I'm old school, note-books and strong verbal communications. Leave the computer for my report writing and our IT lass here."

Holly wasn't quite sure how to take being called a lass, but she kept her mouth shut and prepared to give the new DCI the benefit of any doubt that she might feel about him.

"Right, well let's get started," John shuffled a few papers around and pulled out a typed-up report. "This came in from the SOC team. One thing that particularly interests me is that both men appear to be wearing size 9 shoes with the same tread on the soles and heels. Our key witness, Tom Blair, says that the man he bumped into was wearing what he described as an oil skinned jacket, but I suspect that it was a Barber, popular in England and Europe particularly amongst farmers or country folk. Tom also seemed to think that the man was European when he shouted something like a swear word, but it was not in English. Another witness," here John glanced at his notebook, "a Jen Pate, said that she spoke to a man dressed in what she described as an old blue jacket and she had the impression that they were Dutch. But here's the thing, there were two men together seemingly friends wanting to look at the windmill. The one man introduced himself as Karel and his mate as Gerrit. The witness said that the one man, Karel, did all the talking. So, it looks like we have a dead Dutchman and another on the loose. I've contacted Interpol and asked them to check Airport Control to see if two men named Karel and Gerrit boarded any flights out of Amsterdam in the past couple of weeks. I'm waiting to hear back from them. In the meantime, we are also waiting for the forensics report. I would like you, Sergeant Flowers and Constable Elliot to interview the owner of Windmill Lake Wake and Eco Park and see if they might have a list of all the people who were there during the time of the murder. Constables Brown and Ryan, I would like you to go and interview Tom Blair again and see if he remembers anything else. We have very little to go on here, but someone will have seen something."

Holly put up her hand, "Sir, what about the car? We presume that the two Dutchmen must have driven to Windmill Lake and if they came from Holland it might be that they had rented a car?"

"Good point. Constable, I'll let you look into car rentals booked from Pearson Airport, just see if you can identify a car rented out to two Dutch men. Good, well, it's early days yet but you know what they say about the first twenty-four hours being the most critical in any investigation. Go to it team and we'll meet back here this afternoon at say three o'clock."

There was a hushed silence in the room as the team looked at each other slightly stunned by what DCI Hargreaves had just said. Susan Parker never suggested that they reported twice in a day. It appeared this his new officer was obviously going to be a bit of a slave driver!

NINE

Karel had studied the Vermeer painting in minute detail. *The Milkmaid,* had been painted in 1658 and was one of a series of paintings of women performing everyday activities like pouring milk, trying on pearls, making lace, or playing musical instruments, generally absorbing the life and times of the era in which the women lived. All of the pictures appeared tranquil and, although steeped in realism, portrayed a very gentile way of life.

Karel had run his fingers delicately over the canvas and was amazed at the thickness of the paint and the subtle light which appeared to diffuse the outlines of the depicted scenes yet still managed to use perspective to pull the audience into the main point of view which, in this case was the milkmaid.

What an amazing artist the man had been, Karel thought, yet he had died at only forty-three leaving eleven children, eight of which were still under the age of ten. *I'm almost the same age as Vermeer yet what have I achieved*, Karel mused. He shook his head and then proceeded to carefully roll the canvas up and store it back in the fishing rod case again. *Now what should I do for the rest of the day,* he thought, *and what exactly is my plan of escape?*

Karel decided to go for a walk. He wasn't interested in the shops and this village seemed to have a load of them, mostly dress shops, but he had noticed a fine-looking public library halfway down the main street. Geography had never been his strong point, but he desperately needed a map of the area and Bayfield's proximity to the States. Sure, he could use his smartphone, but somehow looking at maps on a small screen didn't cut it for him. Karel also wanted to check out the marina as that could also be an alternative route to the States.

Leaving the Albion, Karel decided to forgo a visit to the library and focus on a walk to the marina. He checked his phone, pulled up a map of Bayfield and then set off at a brisk pace in the direction of Louisa Street which would take him to Long Hill and then down to the South Shore marina.

It was a fine afternoon with a clear, cobalt blue sky absolutely devoid of any clouds. The humidity of the previous few days had lifted and now the air felt clean and fresh. Walking always helped to clear Karel's head and today was no exception as all the stress of the past days seemed to lift off his shoulders and, for once, Karel felt at peace with the world. Turning on to Louisa Street he continued at a steady pace until he came upon a small cottage the front of which was smothered in honeysuckle. An attractive woman was out front watering her pretty garden, hose pipe in hand and a watering can on the ground beside her. Karel stopped and admired the garden. The woman turned and with her one hand still holding the hose, accidently proceeded to spray water all over Karel.

"Oh my gosh, I'm so very sorry," Kate barked with her loud voice, "You're soaked." She genuinely looked shocked at her mishap, but Karel just laughed saying, "Ah, heck, I'll dry, it's only water and it's a good way to cool me off!"

Kate smiled and went over to shake his hand saying, "That's very big of you, I'm Kate by the way."

"Karel" he answered and went to leave.

"Would you like a drink? I've got a jug of lemonade or you might like a beer? That's the least I can do to make up for the soaking." Kate said.

Karel considered his options. He hadn't been in the company of an attractive woman for a long time and this woman intrigued him with her loud voice and slightly horsey manner.

"Yes, sure, I'd like a beer."

"Come around the back to the patio, just sit down and I'll pop inside and grab a couple of beers. Can or glass?"

Karel looked at her blankly. What did she mean by can or glass? Although his English was exceptionally good, colloquialisms generally had him flummoxed.

Kate could see his confusion and said, "Umm. I meant do you want your beer in a glass or drunk out of a can?"

"Ah, I see, a glass will do nicely, thank you."

They sat out on the patio enjoying the afternoon sun and then Kate broke the silence by saying in her loud voice, "Karel, that's a Dutch name, isn't it?"

Karel nodded thinking this woman was nothing but direct.

"I haven't seen you around the village. Are you just visiting?"

And nosey too, he thought as he decided how much information he should give away and how much to fabricate. The truth was by far the easiest of options, a little bit of truth would do no harm.

"Ya, I'm on holiday from Holland, just here for the next

two days before I head for Michigan. And yourself, how long have you lived here in this charming house?"

Kate found herself telling the strange Dutch man her whole life story concluding with her now new sense of freedom and happiness and her indecision about adopting Lucy, the little fox terrier. Karel laughed when she talked about the dog so earnestly.

"Kate, after all that you've gone through and so much that you've achieved, why would you even hesitate about adopting a little dog?"

"Oh, I know you're right, Karel, I've spent too long second guessing myself over a dog. Thank you, I will go to the animal rescue tomorrow and bring my Lucy dog home."

Karel got up to leave. He had so enjoyed chatting to Kate as she had made him feel quite new and for a brief time, he had been able to forget about everything and enjoy flirting with her. On the spur of the moment he said, "Well, Miss Kate, I will take my leave now, but I would really like to see you again. Would you perhaps join me for dinner tonight at The Albion, say around six-thirty?"

Kate clapped her hands together like a little girl and said, "Oh, yes, that would be lovely. I'll meet you there at six-thirty."

When she smiled, Karel noticed, she had adorable dimples each side of her mouth and her deep blue eyes fairly twinkled. Yes, he definitely liked this woman and thought that he might score well that night.

TEN

J ohn arrived early for their afternoon meeting. The police photographer had sent in a stack of photographs mostly of the dead man, but there were also some of the windmill itself and a few of the lake.

Just what were the two men doing by the lake and more particularly, why were they under the platform of the windmill, John mused as he flicked through the prints one at a time. Dutchmen and windmills went together like a horse and carriage, but what possibly connected these men to the Eco Park?

John picked up the preliminary forensics report and read through the details of the actual murder. Interestingly the bullet that had killed the man was an old one, possibly twenty years old and was not from a gun readily found in North America.

According to forensics the gun had been shot at a very close range to the victims head, no more than a couple of feet away. The body was found underneath the platform and according to the footprints, both men had been standing next to each other. John could visualize the scene, but still, for the life of him, couldn't begin to guess the motive for this murder. Means, motive, and opportunity, the holy grail of any investigation, *but what on earth could the motive be*, he thought.

Sergeant Flowers interrupted John's thoughts by arriving first at the Lion's Hall followed by Constables Elliot, Brown, and Ryan. Soon they were all seated at the long conference table eager to report their findings.

"Okay, good afternoon everyone and a fine one at that, I must say. I have here the photographs taken from the scene of the crime. Could one of you do the honours of taping them up on the board right here. Thank you, Constable Elliot. Right, we can see from this photograph that pretty well the whole of the top of the deceased's head has been blown off. What does that tell us?"

Holly put up her hand.

"It tells us that this guy was shot at close range, sir..."

"Yes. You're quite right and forensics have just confirmed that too. In fact, the gun that fired the bullet killing our man is almost an antique, a Dutch Luger, no longer manufactured and has been out of circulation for a good twenty years. What does that tell us?"

There was silence around the table until Sergeant Flowers spoke, "It could tell us two things, sir, one that the gun was shipped over from Holland maybe twenty years ago or that it was purchased sometime ago probably in Holland. Either way we know that it's of Dutch origin, sir."

"Yes, and seeing that our two men are also Dutch, it does not take a leap of faith to fill in the dots. These men must have brought the gun with them, but how long ago is the question?"

Holly put her hand up, "I think I can answer that question, sir."

"Go ahead, Constable."

"According to Budget Rental, two Dutch men under the names of Karel de Vries and Gerrit Van Heuzen rented a Honda Civic from Pearson Airport on Sunday, July 21st for the duration of ten days. The car rental has details of their flight number, airline, and drivers license number with addresses that I am about to track down through Interpol, but I think we've got him, sir,"

"Well, done, Constable, having the names of both our Dutch men will really help expedite the search. Let's hope that Interpol can come up with something. Now, Constables Elliot and Brown, how did you fair with interviewing our chief witness, what was his name?" John picked up his notebook and flicked through it, "Oh, yes, Tom Blair. Did you find anything of interest?"

Constable Elliot stood up and shuffled his papers before beginning to talk.

"Umm...well, the only added bit of information I got from him is that the Dutch man was carrying a fishing rod case although he had not seen the man actually fishing and that struck him as odd, also he found the man extremely rude, his words were," here Constable Elliot picked up his notes and read verbatim. 'The man pushed past me and muttered something which sounded like a swear word, but in a foreign language. He never apologised and just kept on walking towards the car park.' That's really all I got from him, sir."

"Thank you, Constable."

"Right, in summary we have two Dutchmen arriving at Windmill Lake Wake and Eco Park by means of a car rental from Budget Rental under the names of Karel de Vries and Gerrit Van Heuzen. Approximately thirty minutes later only one Dutch man bumps into Tom Blair and he is carrying a fishing rod case even though there is no evidence that he was actually fishing. He is in a hurry and is heading towards the car park. The second Dutch man is found shortly afterwards with his brains blown out. Now team, we have the means, a Luger, but what we don't have is the motive for this murder. Also, where does the fishing rod case fit into all of this?"

Constable Holly put her hand up, "Sir, maybe the case was used to carry something out of the park?"

John thought for a minute, "What about any witnesses? Did these men have the fishing rod case with them when they first arrived or not? Who interviewed the young woman?" Here John flicked through his notes, "Jen Pate?"

Constable Brown put up his hand and said, "We did interview her and there was no mention of a fishing rod case. We did, however, get a list of people who were wakeboarding, but we haven't been able to interview all of them yet, sir, as some live in Kitchener and one couple were from Sarnia. We managed to interview Rose Blair, she's the wife of our key witness, Tom. She was with their grandchildren who were wakeboarding. Now she observed the two men walking towards the Windmill. She said that they were oddly attired in long, three quarter length jackets which looked out of place in the middle of the summer. That's about all she could contribute as she said she was too busy watching her grandchildren wakeboarding." Constable Brown sat down as John Hargreaves stood up.

"Thanks everyone, you've all done an excellent job. Until we've heard back from Interpol, we won't know who or what we are dealing with. An APS has gone out so the rental car will be tracked down pretty quickly, but my feeling is that our suspect will have long since dumped the car so that won't help us in tracking him down. What I keep coming back to is what on earth were those two oddballs doing at Windmill Lake? What connection is there and what about the fishing rod case? Why carry a case if you are not fishing? Any ideas?"

They seemed to have gone around in circles and judging by the faces of his team they appeared to have hit a blank wall too. It was time to call it a day. He would type up his report and go home, but did he really want to drive back to London, or should he just check into The Little Inn, John thought as he opened up his laptop ready to type. Expenses were covered for all out of town cases so he might just stay a couple of nights locally and that way he could get a feel for the village and maybe subtly ask a few questions too. Yes, he would phone The Little Inn and see if they had a spare room and, with that plan all settled, John began to write up his report.

ELEVEN

As soon as Karel had departed, Kate put her gardening equipment away and then rushed over to see Rose. She had so much to tell her and felt quite giddy with excitement. When was the last time that she had actually been on a date? Bob, her ex, and she had been together since they had been at college which was over forty years ago. There had never been anyone else in her life, indeed, she had never, ever, been to bed with anyone other than Bob and this gave her great pause for thought. Knocking on Rose's front door, Kate suddenly felt overwhelmed. What was she doing going on a date with a strange man, one that she had only just met! Rose opened the door and could immediately tell by her sisters flushed face and agitated demeanour, that something was amiss. "What's wrong, Kate? Come in."

Kate stepped into the hall and started to wring her hands together.

"For God's sake, Kate, what's wrong with you? You look all flushed and anxious. Come on, spill the beans, what have you been up to?"

"Oh, Rose, I've met a man and I'm having dinner with him tonight!"

"Gosh, Kate, that's fantastic. Come on, tell all. Look, I'll put the kettle on for a nice cup of tea."

Rose made the tea and put some freshly made oatmeal cookies onto a plate.

"Let's go on through to the sunroom."

Carrying a tray with two mugs and a teapot, Kate followed Rose carrying the plate of cookies. Ben and Puff were lounging on the sofa together, Puff had his legs in the air and Ben was curled up tightly with his head between his paws.

"Just look at the lazy things," Kate said, "What spoiled puppies,"

Rose smiled and sat down on one of the love seats opposite the dogs who had made no effort to remove themselves from the sofa. She patted the space next to her and Kate joined her, muttering about the dogs being treated like humans, but laughing at the same time.

"Now, how did you meet your man?"

The next ten minutes Kate regaled her sister with the story of how Karel had got soaked and their subsequent beers on the patio. She concluded by saying, "He's not bad looking, a bit younger than me I think, but I like the way he speaks with a slight accent. Honestly, Rose, I know nothing about him, but having dinner with him might shed some more light."

Rose cast a critical look at her sister. She really could do with a good hair cut, she thought, and a general makeover.

"Look, Kate, how about I come over before you go on your date and I can help you get ready. I've got some makeup you can use and what about you wearing my new tunic top. It would fit you nicely."

Just then Tom returned with Abby and Ella chatting nineteen to the dozen about the giant fish they had just seen. He had taken the girls to the beach and then they had walked along the pier. One of the fishermen had just hauled in a huge fish, Tom seemed to think that it was a Perch, but he wasn't totally sure.

"Oh, Aunty Kate, will you play a game with us? We've got Scrabble, Monopoly, or Guess Who."

Tom poured himself a cup of tea and grabbed a handful of cookies. With his mouth stuffed full he said, "Girls, tell grandma and Aunty Kate about the fish that we saw."

Abby clapped her hands together and with an excited voice she said, "Oh, Grandma, we saw a fish this big," and she held her hands out two metres apart. Rose smiled and then, involuntarily a flash went through her mind of the two men she had seen at the Eco Park. Tom had said that one of them had been carrying a fishing rod case, yet she could not recall either of the men holding anything in their hands when they walked passed her. Tom had only seen the one man just before he had discovered the body and he was the man carrying the fishing rod case. If they had not entered the eco park with the case, then that had to mean that the case had been procured somewhere else in the park itself. What was in the fishing rod case and where had it come from in the first place?

"Tom," Rose said, "did the man carrying the fishing rod case look as if he was a fisherman?"

Tom pulled a face and then laughed.

"No, love, now you're asking me a silly question. What does a fisherman look like? Abby and Ella, what does a fisherman look like? We just saw a man pull in a huge fish off the pier. What did he look like?"

Abby and Ella giggled, and Rose laughed with them. Kate looked at them all perplexed as to what was going on.

"Oh, Kate, I'm sorry that we're being somewhat obtuse. I'll tell you all about it later on when I come around to help you get ready for your big date."

With that out of the way Kate took Abby and Ella's hands and walked out into the sunroom where they proceeded to play a game of Scrabble. Rose stood by the sink deep in thought. She would have to speak to the new DCI and tell him about the fishing rod case.

TWELVE

J ohn managed to get a room, the last one available at
The Little Inn. He was upstairs in one of the rooms
that a murder had taken place in two years ago. He
had heard all about it back at The Serious Crimes
Headquarters in London when his boss had handed him a
thick file containing all his predecessor's cases. He had never
personally met DCI Susan Parker, but she was certainly
almost legendary in the department.

Her last case had been the most trying and it was there
with the help of an undercover drug squad officer, that she had
cracked the Mexican cartel drug operation involving the
Mennonites.

It was one of the undercover bikers that the DCI had actually married and was currently on an extended honeymoon in
Tuscany, Italy. The DCI had also been involved in at least six
other different murders all happening in and around the
village of Bayfield, which appeared to be a charming place
seemingly locked in something of a time warp with a wide
main street, trees lining each side and charming shops and

restaurants nestled along rustic sidewalks. It was almost like an English village and John was quite smitten with the charm.

After an exceptionally good meal in The Willow dining room of the Inn, John decided to go for a walk. He always did his best thinking when out and about in the fresh air and he did so want to discover the beach and the marina. He set off at a firm pace heading towards Pioneer Park where he immediately stopped in his tracks and gasped. This was the first time that he had seen Lake Huron in all its glory, and, like most Europeans, his concept of a lake was one that you could see all sides, but here the vastness of the lake was like looking at the ocean. He took in the huge vista and couldn't help but be amazed, Lake Huron was absolutely beautiful. Why, he thought, he could be on the Mediterranean as the water was so azure blue, the sky a cobalt blue and everywhere he looked the water seemed to sparkle like a myriad of diamonds. John walked down the wooden steps to the sandy beach below. He took off his black leather shoes and socks and rolled up his trousers. Walking along the beach and paddling in the clear, sparkling water, he felt as if he was on holiday and for the first time in five years, he could feel the heavy weight that had been burdening his shoulders begin to gently lift. Life felt good once more, very good indeed. John reached the beach car park and sat on a bench to put his shoes and socks back on and then he walked to the end of the pier passing several fishermen with their nets and, here he paused for thought, fishing rod cases? Something still niggled him about the black, cylindrical tube that Tom Blair had mentioned the man, in all likelihood the murderer, had been carrying. What would the murderer be doing with a fishing rod case and where did the case come from in the first place? John let out a deep sigh and shook his head. Enough of speculating, he thought, it was time to relax.

Tomorrow would be another day of investigation, but for now he would just enjoy the beauty of the evening.

Walking back through the car park and seeing all the boats in the marina, he couldn't help but remember the last time that he had been on a sailing boat. Rachel, his daughter, would have only been a young teenager then and Mary had been full of life and healthy too. They had rented a sailboat and taken it out on The Cumberland Basin in Bristol. Rachel had been taking sailing lessons all that summer and had been keen to practice her skills. John remembered the thrill of the sail and how they had all laughed almost hysterically when the boat nearly capsized. These were fine memories, bittersweet and true.

John saw a sign that said, "Mara Street Walkway." It looked like a tunnel of trees ascending a steep foot path to the top of the bluff. He walked up the pathway reaching the top feeling slightly out of breath and realizing that he had actually done a full circle. Pioneer Park was to his right and Main Street straight ahead. He was actually on Bayfield Terrace, which rang a bell. Where had he seen the street name before, John thought. Yes, he remembered, Bayfield Terrace was where his chief witness, Tom Blair, and his wife, Rose, whose name he had also seen when reading through DCI Parker's case histories, lived. He would pay them a brief visit.

THIRTEEN

Rose had just returned from her sister's house where she had helped Kate prepare for her big date. She smiled to herself recalling how nervous her sister had been and how she had given her a pep talk about being open to what may happen. Kate had left to meet her man at The Albion looking very attractive in Rose's turquoise tunic top, cream linen pants with beige strappy sandals, and just the right amount of makeup. She had crossed her fingers and said a quick prayer that everything would work out okay for her sister as she had been through enough and it was time that life threw her a good hand.

Tom had settled Abby and Ella in front of the television, and they were happily watching a *Harry Potter* movie. Rose opened a bottle of wine and beckoned to Tom to join her on the patio. They were just about to go outside when there was a knock on their front door. Rose went to open it and was somewhat taken back by the very tall, handsome man standing on their porch.

"Umm. Yes, how can I help you?" Rose said whilst realization seeped into her consciousness as to whom she was talking to; of course, Tom had mentioned that the new DCI looked like Luther and he most certainly did. In fact, Rose found her heart beating just a little faster and she almost wanted to flutter her eye lids at him.

"I'm sorry to disturb you at this time of night, but I was walking past your house and wondered if I might have a word with your husband. Is he in?"

Rose answered quickly and slightly breathlessly, "Oh, yes, please come in, we were about to have a glass of wine. Would you like to join us on the patio?"

John smiled and followed Rose into a delightfully lovely kitchen where the smell of good, old-fashioned home cooking made his taste buds twitch even though he hadn't long since eaten. This was obviously a kitchen that was much used, and he sensed, much loved. In fact, he had taken an instant liking to Rose Blair and hoped that he could spend some time chatting to her. He walked outside and found himself in a charming walled garden with fruit trees and flowers in abundance. A rambling rose bush tumbled over the stone wall and geraniums cascaded over terracotta pots. Two dogs suddenly came pounding out through the back door and jumped up barking like crazy.

"Puff, Ben shh... this is DCI Hargreaves now be good and settle down."

As if they had understood every word she had spoken, the two dogs obediently went to lie down next to where Tom was sitting. He had stood up when Rose appeared with John and had motioned with his hand for the DCI to take a seat. A tray with a bottle of Cabernet Sauvignon and two wine glasses sat firmly on the glass topped patio table.

"I'll just pop into the kitchen and get another wine glass," Rose said leaving the two men alone on the patio.

Wow, Rose thought, *he's certainly a change from Susan.* She walked over to the mirror in the hallway and looked at herself critically. *What a mess,* she thought, as she rummaged through her purse for a brush and some lipstick. Grabbing a wine glass from the kitchen cabinet, Rose went in to check up on the girls who were totally glued to the television.

"Darlings, do you need anything?" A bowl of popcorn lay half eaten on the coffee table and two glasses of milk sat beside the bowl. Abby turned to Rose and said, "No, thank you Grandma, we're just fine."

"Well, if you want either of us, your grandfather and I are outside on the patio."

Rose left the girls to watch the rather scary movie and went to join the men on the patio. She overheard the DCI ask Tom about the fishing rod case and before she could stop herself Rose interrupted their conversation.

"I wanted to talk to you, Inspector."

John quickly interjected, "Please call me John."

Rose continued, "Umm. John, I've been turning over in my mind that afternoon at Windmill Lake and I do remember seeing the two men walking towards the windmill. They definitely did not have a fishing rod case with them then, I would have noticed it, I'm sure."

Tom interrupted Rose, "Well, I only saw the one man, the one I bumped into, and he was carrying the fishing rod case then."

Rose couldn't stop herself from butting into the conversation, "So, John, where did the man procure the cylindrical case from if he didn't have it with him when the two men arrived? What could be inside the case?"

John laughed, "Now hold your horses, you're jumping to conclusions here. What makes you think that there were not fishing rods inside the case?"

Rose went quiet as she thought, "Yes, you're quite right, I am jumping to conclusions, but it does seem odd that no one saw anyone actually fishing? Oh, well, let's change the subject, John, tell us about yourself. How long have you lived here in Canada?"

John smiled and thought to himself, *she's an attractive woman who speaks her mind, just like my Mary.* He looked up and realized that he hadn't answered her question. "Oh, I'm sorry I was away with the fairies. I've been here for all of two months, well, with the Serious Crimes Squad,

I actually emigrated almost a year ago. I retired from Bristol Serious Crimes Squad after working there for over twenty years. I never had any intention of working again, yet here I am investigating a murder."

"But what brought you to Canada then if it wasn't the work?" Rose asked, intrigued by the man sitting opposite her.

"Ah, well, my daughter married a Canadian chap five years ago. Last year they had their first baby and I decided that I wanted to be a proper grandpa, hence moving to London, Ontario. I actually live just around the corner from my daughter so I get to see little Amelia as often as I can, and she is perfect."

Rose wanted to know if there was a Mrs. Hargreaves, but she didn't quite know how to ask. Tom, on the other hand had no qualms in just blurting out, "What about your wife? Is she with you in London?"

John went very quiet and for a moment Rose thought that he was not going to answer Tom.

"Umm. Mary passed away just after Rachael got married

five years ago. She got to see our beautiful daughter walk down the aisle, but never saw her granddaughter who, incidentally, looks the spitting image of her." John's voice quavered a bit and Rose gently put her hand on his shoulder.

"I'm so very sorry for your loss, John, you must miss her dreadfully."

"Thank you, Rose. Yes, not a day goes by that I don't think of her." He coughed and cleared his throat before continuing, "After Mary died, I lost all motivation to work and decided to retire from the police force. Rachael had moved to Canada, so it made sense for me to follow her and here I am working again and beginning to feel that life has some meaning after the darkness of the past five years. What about you two? How long have you been living here in Bayfield?"

Rose answered before Tom could get a word in. "We moved here twelve years ago, although Tom's family had a cottage on Pavilion Road which we sometimes visited. Living here in the village is marvelous. It was the best move that we've ever made, moving here."

John swigged back his glass of wine and made to leave. "Well, I've taken up enough of your time and I really do need to get back to The Little Inn and review my notes. We're still waiting on Interpol to get back to us and hopefully by tomorrow we might know just who we're dealing with and possibly be enlightened as to the motivation behind the murder. Thank you both for the wine."

"John, you must come for dinner one evening. I'll get word to you as soon as I've had the chance to look at my planner. Our granddaughters are going back to Montreal on Wednesday so maybe sometime after that?"

"That would be splendid. It has been so nice to have met

you both." John waved as he walked down the drive and onto Bayfield Terrace.

Tom turned to Rose and said, "That's one nice guy, but his eyes looked so sad."

Yes, Rose thought, *he appeared to be carrying the world on his shoulders.* She would have to try to help lift the weight, somehow.

FOURTEEN

Kate had stood outside The Albion in a bit of a dither totally undecided as to whether to go inside or wait for Karel to appear. In the end she entered the pub and looked around to see if he was already waiting for her. Suddenly, she felt a tap on her shoulder and there he was with a big smile on his face.

"You showed up, Kate, I wasn't sure if you would come. May I say that you look lovely tonight."

Kate smiled and inwardly thanked her sister for sprucing her up for this date.

They were shown to their table and soon drinks arrived in front of them. Karel appeared much more relaxed then previously and Kate soon found herself relaxing too. By the end of the evening Karel took her hand and said in a husky voice, "Kate, would you come up to my room for a drink before going home?"

Kate was a little taken aback by Karel's directness and then she remembered her sister telling her to be open, besides she could feel a little tinkling in her body which felt exciting and could not, or should not, be ignored.

She looked at her watch and pointedly said, "Sure, Karel, I'd love to have a night cap, but I can't be too late; I'm at the animal rescue tomorrow morning."

Karel got up and, taking her hand, he led her to the stairs leading to the bedrooms above. His room was situated at the front of The Albion and had a balcony that overlooked Main Street. The room was really quite spartan, but clean with a queen bed in the middle, a large digital wall television and a chest of drawers. There was a small bathroom, no bigger than a wardrobe, just off the bedroom. They both sat on the bed and suddenly Kate felt decidedly uncomfortable and awkward. Karel put his arm around her shoulders and pulled her into a passionate embrace which had her almost gasping for air. Karel started to pull at her clothing and began to breathe hard and fast. Kate wasn't sure how to react. It had been two years since she had sex and that had been with Bob and hadn't exactly been passionate. After thirty-five years of an intimate relationship with just one man she had forgotten how to respond to another man's advances. She let out a deep sigh and pushed Karel away, "I don't think that I'm ready yet for this, Karel."

"Would another glass of wine help relax you?" Karel said almost pleadingly. Kate could see that he was highly turned on and seeing his bulging pants made her feel a little turned on herself. She nodded her head and whispered, "Yes, maybe another glass of wine will do the trick."

Karel kissed her and said that he would be just five minutes, as long as it took to pop downstairs to the bar and buy a bottle of wine and bring it back to the room.

As soon as he had left, Kate got up and straightened the tunic top feeling indecisive as to whether she should take the opportunity to remove all her clothes and hop into bed naked or to take flight and go back home. She glanced around the room and noticed a fishing rod case. *Funny*, she thought, *Karel hadn't mentioned that he was a fisherman.* Bob, her ex, had loved to fish, mostly salmon, so Kate knew a thing or two about fishing. She unzipped the case and peered inside expecting to see several rods, but there was nothing inside. She peered again and put her hand into the case feeling the insides. She felt some sort of fabric and was just about to pull it out when the bedroom door opened. Kate pushed the fabric back inside the case and quickly zipped it up. She stood up and smiled at Karel who had entered carrying a bottle of wine and two glasses. Kate went to him and taking the bottle and glasses out of his hands she wrapped her arms around and drew him to her body, whispering in his ear, "Take me, Karel, I'm ready."

FIFTEEN

DCI Hargreaves woke up early and went down to the Tap Room at The Little Inn for his breakfast. He opened up his laptop to check if there had been anything back from Interpol and to his relief, sure enough, there was an email. He quickly opened and scanned the contents. *Well, well,* John thought, *all was revealed with one click of the mouse.* This information would help the case tremendously and he could hardly wait to reveal all to his team. Finishing off his breakfast and gulping down the last dregs of his coffee, John set off at a fast pace in the direction of the Lion's Hall. As he walked past the shop called Shop Bike, the strong aroma of freshly ground coffee assaulted his senses. He could see quite a cluster of people gathering inside and standing on the wooden deck. Some were sitting on Muskoka chairs lined up on the sidewalk, which he found quite charming. Further, on a tall, wooden carving of a sailor wearing a bright yellow sou'wester stood by the entry to a lovely looking black and white patio with a sign above saying, Drift. Comfortable patio furniture, tables, and chairs adorned the space with ferns and other plants dotted around. The Black Dog, next door to Drift, John had observed the previous evening, had appeared to be the most popular of all the eating establishments in the village, as long lines of people cued up to get seats. It looked to be an attractive bistro style restaurant with a good ambiance and patio space. John ear marked it as a place to visit along with the small restaurant, Drift.

He reached The Lion's Hall a good twenty minutes before the rest of the team which gave him time to get his thoughts together. It was one thing knowing who and what it was they were up against, but quite another thing, how to proceed with that knowledge.

Constable Holly arrived first and said a chirpy "Good morning, guv," while proceeding to open up her laptop and tap in her password. "Ah, here it us, guv. I downloaded an article written all about the Windmill. It's quite informative and gives the whole history and background of the development."

John was amused at being called guv, but he chose not to say anything as he liked the young, fresh faced, eager Constable who was an obvious whiz on computers, and he most certainly didn't want to get her back up. He glanced at the online article and remarked out loud, "Gosh, some parts of the lake are more than forty-five feet deep, and the lake is named Roleka. I knew that it was manmade but didn't know that it was actually thirty-five acres of water."

They were interrupted by the voices of the rest of the team arriving all of whom came in carrying cups of coffee with the word Shop bike scrawled across. Sergeant Flowers handed a cup to John saying, "Here you are, sir, compliments of Shop Bike. Leanne and Shawn said, 'Welcome to Bayfield.'"

John smiled and took the cup of coffee graciously although

he rarely drank more than one cup a day and had already consumed that at breakfast.

"Okay, everyone, it's time to roll. I have received a response back from Interpol and it appears that our two Dutchmen are, as suspected, on the radar. Karel de Vries and the deceased, Gerrit Van Heuzen have spent the past twenty years incarcerated at Amsterdam Penitentiary. They are both petty thieves but had moved into high-end art theft and forgery. In fact, according to Interpol, they had quite the operation going employing a master painter whose work was so good that many of his reproductions had been authenticated by some of the world's leading auction houses and passed with flying colours as being the real deal. There are, apparently, few such master painters and their trick is using the original method of painting with hand made and ground pigments. The trio was caught trying to sell a Vermeer to an undercover art dealer in Michigan. They were put away for twenty years and released just one year ago. So, the million-dollar question is what were two of them doing in Bayfield, in particular at Windmill Lake? It does appear, according to Interpol, that Karel and Gerrit visited Canada not long before they were caught. What they were doing here we have yet to discover. Right, you lot, any thoughts?"

There was silence in the room as the team digested the information. Sergeant Flowers put up his hand. "How did they pass on the forged paintings? Did they have dealers requesting certain paintings and if so, were they also in on the forgeries, sir?"

John looked at the report from Interpol and shook his head saying, "No, unfortunately there's not much information here other than the bare facts. Maybe that is something that you could research, Constable Ryan, lists of dealers connected to Karel and Gerrit."

Constable Ryan put her hand up, "I'll also see if any other paintings went missing just before the men came to Canada twenty-two years ago. You see, guv, it could be that a painting taken out of its frame could easily be rolled up and hidden inside a fishing rod case. Engineers and architects use similar tube containers to hold their drawings so why not use a fishing rod case to store a canvas in?"

John nodded eagerly, "Now you're thinking. Yes, yes, you could very well be right. What if twenty-two years ago they hid the painting in the fishing-rod case, brought it to Canada and ended up hiding it away under the windmill. They were arrested just after returning from Canada and maybe, just maybe, they came back to retrieve the painting after being released from jail. I think we're onto something here."

Constable Elliot interrupted, "But why bring the painting to Canada in the first place, sir?"

John paused for thought before replying, "If your theory is right, Constable Ryan, there would records of any painting that had been stolen and not found in the past twenty-two years. We should be starting on that premise and working backwards from that point. Whatever, we still have a killer loose in the community. Have we managed to find the rental car yet?"

Constable Elliot replied, "We've put out an alert for the car, no results yet, sir."

"Constables Brown and Elliot check all the motels, inns, and hotels in the area and see if any Dutch men have checked in. Of course, he could be far away by now or he could be just laying low. Don't forget, if your theory is correct and he has procured the painting to either sell or move on, that will significantly dictate his moves. Right, I'll leave you to your searches. Be back here by two this afternoon."

The team shuffled out of the room leaving John to type up his report to the head office. They still had far too many loose ends and the case already felt as if it was losing momentum and was beginning to go cold before it had even started. John let out a deep sigh and began to type up his report.

SIXTEEN

"*Potverdore!*" Karel muttered. "*Potverdore*, that nosey bitch looking in the fishing-rod case." She thought that he hadn't seen her, but he had and now she was definitely a liability. Much as he had enjoyed their romp in the bed together and, yes, she had been like a ripe peach, oh so sweet, juicy, and quite delectable to eat, but business was business and nothing could jeopardize his plans. Anneka, his girlfriend, would soon be joining him and then he would dispose of the painting. First, though, he would have to deal with Kate. Her death must be made to look like an accident, perhaps a drowning in the lake? Yes, he liked the idea of going for a romantic swim and then accidently pushing Kate under the water. The more he contemplated this idea the better it sounded. It would also kill two birds with one stone as he had promised to be in touch with her that day. He would suggest a romantic picnic on the beach followed by a swim in the lake and that would be that. He would contact Kate immediately and put his plan into action.

Kate had left The Albion at around one that morning. She

had walked sleepily home hoping that no one would see her as she felt as if everyone would be able to tell that she was absolutely shagged out. Her lips felt bruised and her body tingled all over making her feel weak at the knees. She couldn't remember the last time that she had been brought to multiple orgasms; she involuntarily shuddered just remembering her climaxes. Yes, he was good, the Dutchman, very, very good in bed, although there was something about him that didn't sit well with Kate. Maybe it was because he had not been very sensitive to her vulnerability. He never once asked if she was okay although he did know a thing or two about how to please a woman. She couldn't wait to crawl into her bed and relive the whole sensation of being caressed from her head to her toes by an expert love maker. What would her sister think? Kate thought, *I truly feel like a wanton woman, and she chuckled to herself.* She opened her front door and with no further ado, climbed into bed fully clothed, and fell into a deep, deep sleep only to be awakened six hours later by the shrill sound of the phone ringing in her ears. It was Rose wanting to know all about her date.

Rose herself, had been up since dawn. She hadn't slept at all well and the only thing that helped was cooking; it was like therapy to Rose. She decided to make some almond croissants and some chocolate muffins for breakfast. Jessica would be arriving later on that morning to pick up the girls and she would pack up a bag of goodies for them to munch on the long journey back up to Montreal.

Grabbing a mixing bowl and glancing at the clock which read five thirty, Rose started to make the almond paste which would go inside the croissants. She had bought a couple of Pillsbury Croissant tubes which made making the pastries really easy. She used ground almonds, icing sugar, and egg whites to bind everything into a paste. Then rolled it all out and put in the fridge to chill while the croissant pastry was prepared. She cut small pieces of the chilled paste and then rolled them inside the pastry, finally putting the whole tray into a hot oven to bake. Then Rose turned her hand to making the chocolate muffins. She would add big chunks of chocolate, not just the chips, as she really liked her muffins to be rich and chocolatey. By the time Abby and Ella appeared, the breakfast table was set with two plates mounded high with almond croissants and chocolate muffins. Rose placed a glass of milk in front of each little girl and then told them to dig in. Tom appeared bleary eyed and put the coffee on whilst eyeing the food on the table.

"Oh, Tom, good, you're up. I'm going to take a couple of these pastries around to Kate's house. Can you stay and watch the girls until I get back?"

Tom looked at his watch and yawned. It was only eight o'clock. He had planned to play golf with Doug at ten.

"Sure, Rose, but I am playing golf at ten."

"Okay, darling, I'll be back no later than nine thirty. Don't forget that Jessica will be here around lunch time. I'm sure that she'll want to see you."

Tom looked doubtful. Last time he had seen their daughter they had had a fearful argument and Jessica had stalked off in a huff. It was normally Rose and their daughter who walked a prickly path, not him, and it had made Tom feel distinctly uncomfortable.

"Well my game will last at least two hours, probably more. I'll try to get back in time, but I'm not making any promises. She'll stay on for lunch, won't she?"

"Oh yes," Rose said, "She's visiting friends in Toronto

tonight before heading back home. I suspect she'll leave here around three."

"Not good timing if you ask me, she'll hit the rush hour traffic alright." Tom muttered as he sat down with Abby and Ella and proceeded to help himself to a muffin. He actually would have preferred bacon and eggs for breakfast but knew that Rose had made the pastries and muffins especially for the girls.

"Right, see you later, darling," Rose left quickly carrying a paper bag containing a couple of almond croissants and muffins.

Kate had just finished showering when her sister arrived and knocked loudly on the door. Wrapping a large, fluffy towel around her body, she padded to the door and let Rose in.

"Hey, you look all pink and glowing," Rose said and walked into the kitchen. "I've brought breakfast, now I'll make the coffee while you get yourself dressed."

Kate did as she was told thinking to herself that Rose never changed, still the bossy older sister, but one with a big heart. Ten minutes later the two sisters sat comfortably on the sofa, steaming mugs of coffee in hand and croissants half eaten.

"So, tell all, I can't wait to hear how your date went!"

"Well..." And Kate told Rose everything, although a slightly edited version leaving out the rampant sex. She couldn't understand, though, why Rose jumped up with excitement when she described the fishing rod case.

"What are you so excited about, Rose? I know it was weird having an empty fishing rod case and yes, there was definitely some sort of cloth or canvas tucked inside, but it's no big deal!"

Rose was almost beside herself; she would have to get immediately in touch with DCI Hargreaves. It looked as if they had found the mystery fishing rod case.

SEVENTEEN

The previous afternoon had found the team very much in low spirits. Constable Ryan was still researching art dealers in Europe and North America and had contacted the Rijks Museum in Amsterdam. They had assured her that they would look into stolen paintings from twenty-two years ago. Constable Ryan also requested a list of paintings that had been restored in the past. This, too, she was waiting for the results.

Sergeant Flowers had tracked down the Budget Rental car which had been left and found in the Bayfield Marina car park, but other than that the investigation had ground to a halt. DCI Hargreaves had suggested that Constables Brown and Elliot show the photograph of Karel de Vries to all the retailers and restaurants down Bayfield Main Street and, if needed, to conduct a house to house showing of the photograph to try to track down the murderer.

Now, the following day, the team seemed more energized and pepped up. Constable Ryan had narrowed the list of art dealers and buyers in Ontario around 1996 to 1997, and there were only four who dealt primarily with the old Dutch masters. She also researched buyers in Michigan around the same time and only came up with two. Of the six dealers, only three were still in business and she had the addresses of them, but just waited further instruction from her boss as to how to proceed with this information.

Constables Elliot and Brown had shown the photograph of Karel de Vries to everyone down the Main Street and several people said that they thought that they had seen the man, but it was at The Albion where they really struck gold. Yes, they had had a man named Karel de Vries staying for three days, but he had just checked out that morning. One of the bar tenders had observed Karel go upstairs with a woman the previous night and another staff member remembered seeing a woman creep out of the building at around one in the morning. When the manager was asked if he had seen what car the man had been driving, they had drawn a blank. No one had actually seen him leave, but when he checked out at the desk, he had been carrying a fishing rod case with him.

"Okay, team, this man has wheels from somewhere or someone, we need to find him and find him fast."

Just then John's cell phone rang. It was Rose Blair.

EIGHTEEN

After her sister left, Kate had got herself ready to go to the animal rescue where she volunteered. She was just tidying away the breakfast things, collecting the coffee mugs, and wiping away the crumbs left on the table from the flaky, but delicious croissants, when the phone rang. It was Karel.

"Kate, you disappeared on me without saying goodbye. Look, I really would love to see you again. Do you like the idea of a picnic by the lake followed by a swim? It's very hot today, I believe around thirty degrees and the lake looks so very enticing. Please say yes."

Kate thought about it for a minute. She could easily phone the animal rescue and reschedule her visit and yes, it was going to be a real scorcher today and a swim did sound lovely. She made up her mind and replied quickly, "Yes, I would love to join you Karel. What time?"

"My car is playing up, could you pick me up at about ten. I'll be waiting for you outside The Albion. See you soon."

Kate looked at the clock. It was already gone nine-thirty.

Oh well, she thought, *I'll just go with the flow and enjoy the day.* Grabbing her swimming costume and towel, Kate then went back to her bedroom to put some makeup on and to change her underwear into something a bit sexier than her granny knickers and Playtex bra. Kate looked at her body critically in the mirror and came to the conclusion that she would really have to go on a diet and maybe work out again. She let out a sigh and gathered everything into a large tote bag and headed out to meet her date.

He was waiting outside The Albion with a small rucksack and the fishing rod case. Kate must have registered some surprise as he opened the passenger door and placed the rod case on the seat alongside his rucksack. There was no sign of a picnic.

"Umm. What is all of this, Karel and where's the picnic?"

"I thought that we could swing by the supermarket and pick up some sandwiches and fruit and maybe something to drink."

Kate shrugged her shoulders, "Okay, but what's with the fishing rod case, are you planning to catch some fish?" She almost said, the case with no fishing gear, but stopped herself in time.

"Oh, just in case I have time to fish. Now, enough questions, it's a beautiful day, let's just enjoy a swim and a picnic and maybe recapture some of last night's magic."

Kate smiled and drove off towards the supermarket.

After buying a couple of packs of sandwiches, two bottle of fruit juice and some apples, they headed back to Kate's car.

"Okay, Karel, where shall we go?"

He looked at her blankly before saying smoothly, "This is your territory, where do you recommend we go for a quiet swim?"

Kate thought for a minute. Pavilion Road beach just south of the village, would fit the bill as not only was there a quiet beach, but there was also a washroom where she could change into her swimsuit.

"Right, I know just the place."

Five minutes later found the car parked and Karel and Kate standing in the picnic pavilion.

"I think that I'll change into my bathing suit up here, Karel." Kate said and proceeded to enter the Ladies washroom. Soon they were both walking down the wooden steps to the small, but sandy beach below. Karel laid out two towels and patted one for Kate to join him.

"Race you to the water," he said and jumped up running to the lake with Kate following a few metres behind. The previous year the lake had been really high leaving very little beach, but this year the water level was lower and as a result Pavilion beach stretched along the shore from the bottom of the bluff, a good fifty feet to the water's edge.

Kate laughed as Karel lunged at her splashing his strong legs in the air and grabbing her legs in what she thought was a playful motion. She was thrown backwards into the water and jumped back up gasping for air. Karel looked at her strangely and suddenly Kate felt alarm bells going off inside her head as he lunged once more, and she managed to sidestep him. One thing Karel did not know and that was Kate was a very strong swimmer. She had actually held a gold medal for swimming back in Kelowna all those years ago. But the big question was, was Karel just being playful or was there something more sinister about his intent? She glanced at his face and she suddenly felt her skin prickle with fear. Here, on this deserted beach, anything could happen. Kate decided that she should go with her intuition and without further ado, as he lunged at her for the third time, she turned, and, using a strong crawl stroke, she swam away from him. Seconds later he started to swim after her, but she was by far the stronger swimmer of the two and soon he was way in the distance, and she was miles from shore. Kate saw him turn from her and swim back towards the beach and then she could just about see him walking up the steps to the top of the bluff. She turned and started to swim with all her might back to the shore, but just as she clambered out of the water, the sound of her car revving made Kate jolt. She ran to the towel and looked for her purse which she knew she had left by the tote bag. It wasn't there. She ran over to the wooden stairs and began ascending them with a heavy feeling sitting at the pit of her stomach. Sure enough, her car was gone and her purse too. She didn't know what felt worse the fact that she had been conned so easily by thinking Karel was taking her out on a hot date, or that he had used her to steal a car, not to mention attempting to drown her. *Darn*, she thought as she walked to the nearest house on Pavilion Road and knocked on the door. What had she done getting involved with a rotten man like Karel? She prayed that her sister Rose would be in.

NINETEEN

The team awaited DCI Hargreaves wondering where the normally punctual man could be. The past few days had shown him to be a meticulous and conscientious man, exacting and thorough in his approach to the investigation. It was therefore with some relief that they saw him enter the Lion's Hall fifteen minutes later.

"Sorry everyone, I got detained by a very distressed woman, Rose Blair, who first of all phoned me early this morning to report that her sister had seen the fishing rod case in the bedroom of none other than our man, Karel de Vries. As we now know he was booked into The Albion and had stayed there three days before, checking out early this morning. I was about to head out to come here when I received another call from Rose Blair saying that her sister, Kate, had her car stolen and her purse too and Karel de Vries was the perpetrator. Apparently, they had gone for a picnic to Pavilion Beach. She claims that he attempted to drown her and that she managed to swim away. It was then that he hot footed it to the shore, absconding with her car keys and purse, and drove off in her car leaving a very angry and upset Kate behind. She phoned her sister, who phoned me, and so now we have the car's license plate number. I've sent out an APB to all the OPP detachments in the area."

Constable Elliot put up his hand to speak, "Sir, I was just going to report that the Budget Rental car has been located."

"Where, Constable?" DCI Hargreaves asked.

"It was parked down in the North Shore Marina car park."

"Oh, thank you, Constable, at least that ties up that lose end. Right, well, in summary we have Karel de Vries entering the country with Gerrit Van Heuzen where the two men appear to have rented a car from Budget at Pearson International Airport. They then proceed to drive all the way to Bayfield and seemingly make a beeline for Windmill Lake. Now this is purely speculation, but it looks like the men might have hidden something in the fishing rod case and proceeded to stash it away underneath the windmill the last time they had visited the site over twenty-two years ago. So, they come back to retrieve this fishing-rod case and Karel decides, for some, reason to murder his friend Gerrit and then to scarper off with the case on his own.

"We then have Karel checking in to The Albion where he appears to have stayed for three days, sometime of which he met Rose Blair's sister, Kate. Seemingly they had dinner together, went back to his room where she happened to see the fishing rod case and being nosey, she looks inside and sees nothing, which she is surprised at, but puts her hand inside and feels some sort of fabric. The next day Karel and Kate drive out to Pavilion Beach to have a picnic and go for a swim. He attempts to drown her and then leaves her stranded by stealing her car and purse. Whatever is in the fishing rod case must be worth killing for as it all seems rather extreme to murder first, his partner, Gerrit Van Heuzen, and then second, an attempt to murder Rose Blair's sister."

Constable Ryan put up her hand, "I suppose forty million dollars might be a suitable motivation for murder, guv."

DCI Hargreaves's jaw dropped, "What have you got for us, Constable?"

"Well, I've been researching famous Dutch painters and looking to see if any have gone missing. There is one in dispute, and it's called *The Milkmaid* by Vermeer. Apparently, it has been authenticated by several different auction houses, including Sotheby's, and has been declared the real deal. A forensic art specialist, Dr. Moleevaar from Zaandam in Holland, claims that although the paint and pigments used in the execution of the painting are exactly the same as those used in the seventeenth century by Vermeer, the actual canvas that the painting was conducted on is that of a modern-day thread. The Rijks Museum will not acknowledge that they might have a forgery hanging on their walls, so the case is still in dispute. But, sir, if *The Milkmaid*, in the museum is not the real painting then it begs the question, where is the authentic one? Could it be rolled up and stuffed in the fishing rod case, sir?"

John nodded thoughtfully, "Right, well it seems even more imperative that we apprehend Karel de Vries as soon as possible. My guess is that he will be desperate to sell this painting to a dealer and fast. Constable Ryan, you have the list of art dealers and buyers here in Ontario and in Michigan? Get on to them straight away. Take Constable Elliot with you and don't let them know that you're coming. In fact, go as a surveillance team and keep tabs on their every move. If Karel is going to make contact with any of them, he'll be doing it soon. His return air tickets are for two days time although he must know that we would be watching the airport and looking out for him at all border crossings.

"Keep up the good work everyone. We are closing in on the man, I can feel that the net is tightening. Right, I need to go and interview Rose Blair's sister, Kate, and see if there is anything to add that I've missed out."

TWENTY

As soon as Rose had got the panic phone call from Kate, she had bundled Abby and Ella into her old beat up Volvo, scribbled a short note to Jessica should she arrive while they were out, and had driven a bit like a mad thing to Pavilion Road. There Kate sat forlornly under the roof of the pavilion and immediately Rose's heart went out to her.

"Abby and Ella just stay in the car while I go and talk to your Aunty Kate."

"Why, Grandma, can't we go down to the beach?"

"Not right now, darling, your mom will be waiting and your uncle Paul and Atzuko are bringing baby Yuki to see you both, so I'll be very quick and then we'll go home. Okay?"

"Okay." They both said in unison.

Kate had stood up and started to walk towards them and Rose could see that her face was flushed and her eyes red from crying. She wore only a towel wrapped around her swimming costume, fortunately it was a scorching hot day and she was almost dry.

"Rose, oh Rose, that bastard tried to kill me." Kate's, normally strong, loud, barking voice had been reduced to a harsh whisper. Big, fat glistening tears started to roll down her cheeks and she brushed them away fiercely with the back of her hand.

"I'm such a fool. I thought that we had a thing going on and instead he was just using me."

Rose put her arms around her sister's shoulders and pulled her into a tight hug. "Poor thing, you've been through hell. Now listen, I've called DCI Hargreaves and he wants to speak to you, but before he does, you need to go home, have a stiff drink and get yourself dressed. Jessica and Paul will be here soon so I'll drop you off at your house first and you can walk around when you feel up to it, or you can come home with me and I can lend you some clothes to wear." Rose kissed her sister gently on her cheek and started to walk towards her car where two anxious little faces were peering out at their aunty with unbridled curiosity.

"Is Aunty Kate crying?" Ella asked in her very precise way of talking.

"Oh, she's just a bit sad as someone stole her car and you know how much she loves her car." Rose prefabricated liberally while Kate sniffed loudly and got into the car, bravely smiling at her two nieces. They were soon driving back down Highway 21 heading for the village of Bayfield and home.

Sure enough Jessica had already arrived and was in the house playing with Puff and Ben when Rose pulled up the drive.

"Hi, Mom, is Dad out? Hallo, my muffins." Abby and Ella ran to their mother and gave her a big hug. It had only been a week since they had last seen their mom, but they had missed her. Jessica untangled herself from the girls and said, "Is Paul coming over with Atsuko and the baby, Mom?"

Rose answered yes and hurried Kate through into their bedroom.

"Mom, why is Aunt Kate half dressed? What's going on?"

Abby piped up, "Aunty Kate was crying."

Rose closed the bedroom door leaving Kate to change and then she beckoned her daughter into the kitchen. With a quiet voice she told Jessica about the near drowning and car theft. "So you see, darling, she's a little bit shaken. Just give her a few minutes to compose herself and she'll be okay."

Jessica nodded and went into the sun lounge where the two girls were sprawled on the love seat.

"Okay you two monkeys, what have you been up to?"

TWENTY-ONE

K arel had driven to Clinton in Kate's car where he pulled into the busy car park at the Clinton Slots. Taking out his phone he called Anneka.

"*Wat doe je nom?*" he fairly shouted, meaning where are you now?

Anneka had been travelling for almost twelve hours straight and was totally exhausted. All she wanted to do was to check into a hotel, have a hot shower and creep into bed. She was so sleep deprived that she should not have been driving, particularly in a foreign country and in a rental car at that. She did, however, love Karel with all her heart and knew that he would be feeling frantic by now. Making herself calm down, taking a deep breath, she anxiously willed Karel to calm down saying, "Whatever Karel, you must not draw any attention to yourself. Now you say that you're parked in a busy car park so this is the time to ditch the car and get another. Is there a motel near where you are?"

"Ya, there is one in the next town called The Blyth Inn. They only have seven rooms, so I've already booked one under the name of Gert Van Dupre. Anneka, when will you be here?"

Karel sounded just like a little boy, with his petulant childish voice and he was just that, a little boy, well at least in her minds eye. Anneka could remember him thirty years ago when he was just ten and she was eight, the same pleading voice begging her to come over to his house to play. Then that same voice five years later, only somewhat huskier, begging for sexual favours and then, only five years later, Karel pleading for her to visit him in jail. Somehow, she had not succeeded in quelling his need and dependence on her to always come to his rescue when the going got tough. It was time, though, time to move on and be rid of all his pleading once and for all.

Karel grabbed the fishing rod case and his small rucksack and slowly got out of the car where he proceeded to walk up and down the car park surreptitiously looking into the cars parked outside the casino. Finally he found a pale blue Toyota Corolla left with its car keys still in the ignition. He opened the car and slid quickly into the driver's seat. Soon he was driving on Highway 4 heading in the direction of Blyth.

It was a beautiful day with an azure blue sky occasionally punctuated with little puffs of clouds. Within minutes Karel found himself driving through rural Huron County at its finest, slowing down only as he approached a small settlement called Londesborough. Ten minutes later he found himself outside an unexpected eye catching, yet somewhat incongruous, glass barn-like building called Cowbell. This apparently was a brewery, an ultra modern beer house, bigger indeed then any that he had seen even in Amsterdam. Much as he would have loved to have stopped to sample the beer, Karel drove on until he came to his destination, The Blyth Inn. The lobby of the inn was all fieldstone with a bar and pool table to one side and the bedrooms up the stairs. He had registered as Gert Van Dupre and had paid cash for the room. As soon as he entered his bedroom, he kicked off his boots, threw down his rucksack and jumped on to the bed where he lay spread eagled with total abandonment. He would sleep and then wait for his darling Anneka to arrive.

TWENTY-TWO

Rose and Tom stood at their front door waving a final goodbye to their son, Paul, Atsuko, and baby Yuki. *Talk about a busy afternoon*, Rose thought as they closed the front door and retreated into their living room.

Tom turned to Rose and said, "A sherry, love?" He was a mind reader, Rose thought as she had just been thinking that she needed something a bit stronger than a cup of tea having spent a couple of hours with noisy grandchildren, a baby crying, and her depressed sister all rolled into one. *Oh, for a quiet life*, Rose thought. Tom had ambled in after his game of golf to find Jessica and the girls getting ready to leave and Paul and Atsuko trying to sooth a crying baby.

He almost turned around to walk right back the way he had come had Rose not caught him at the front door. She had hissed at him, "Tom, it's your turn to take the baby," and by the fraught looks on everyone's faces he had no choice but to cradle baby Yuki in his arms.

"I think that I'll take him outside into the garden, love, give you all a little break." The relief was palpable, Rose had put the kettle on to make some tea, Jessica and the girls had decided to stay on a little longer, and Paul and Atsuko began to unwind a little. Kate, on the other hand, had seemed to grow more morose as the afternoon progressed and had already made her excuses for going back to her own house as much to escape the pandemonium as to nurse her own bruised ego.

"So, Mom, what was that all about with Aunty Kate?" Jessica asked as she ambled into the kitchen and leaned against the sink watching her mother putting cookies on a plate.

Rose looked a little flustered, "Well, I told you about the near drowning and car theft, but what I didn't say was this man had dated your aunt and made her feel special. She feels used and abused now and coming so soon after Uncle Bob left her, well, she's naturally suffered a big blow to her self-esteem."

Jessica nodded and said, "But who would steal a car, mom, particularly around here? Sure, in Montreal it's common enough, but here in Huron County?"

"Well, the police are on to it," and, as if on cue, the telephone rang. It was DCI Hargreaves wanting to speak to Rose.

"Hallo, Rose, I just wanted you to know that we've found your sister's car. I realized that for some reason I only have your contact details in my notebook so I hope that you won't mind letting your sister know."

Rose smiled, "Oh, that's such wonderful news. Kate will be absolutely thrilled. I'm assuming that the man who almost drowned my sister and stole her car is the same man whom we saw at the windmill? You know, the man who was carrying the fishing rod case."

Jessica looked at her mother aghast. Rose put her finger to her mouth to prevent her from saying anything as she hadn't finished her conversation with John.

"I've been thinking about what Kate said about some material being rolled up inside the case. Could it be a map, maybe a canvas, or some sort of drawing?"

John laughed and then said, "You know, Rose, I cannot discuss the investigation with you, but needless to say we are researching all possibilities including your theory."

Rose had heard her friend DCI Susan Parker repeat the same thing to her on countless occasions and she knew the solution. "Umm. John, would you like to come for dinner tomorrow night? Please say yes."

"Well, that would be lovely, thank you. I'll bring a bottle of wine. What time do you want me?"

"Oh, six would be great."

John thought for the hundredth time how early people ate their dinner in Canada. Back in the U.K. if he had been invited to a dinner party it would have never been before eight o'clock and the same with booking a restaurant. However, he had been charmed by the complete warmth of all the Canadians he had met and if eating early was just one of the things he had to put up with then that was nothing compared to the welcoming he just knew that he would receive.

As soon as Rose put the phone down Jessica turned on her mother angrily, "Mom, please don't tell me that you're actually involved with that murder out at Windmill Lake?"

"How do you know about that, darling?" Rose asked innocently.

"I do watch the news, Mom, so I know that a body was found underneath the platform of the windmill at the Wakeboard Eco Park. Didn't you take Abby and Ella wakeboarding there the other day?"

Rose gulped and looked guiltily at the floor.

"Mom, don't tell me that was the actual day of the murder? What is it with you? How many more murders are you going to get mixed up in? You know that you almost died two years ago!"

"Jessica, I don't go looking for all of this you know, it just happens that I appear to be in the wrong places at all the wrong times, that's all!"

Tom entered the kitchen just then and stood there wryly looking at his wife and their daughter. He could immediately see by her body language and the thunderous look on her face that there had been some sort of confrontation. Yuki was still cradled in his arms fast asleep and so he carried the sleeping baby back to Atsuko and Paul saying, "Here you are, loves, where shall I put him?"

"Could you lay him on your bed, Dad?" Paul said getting up and following his dad into the bedroom where Tom gently placed Yuki in the middle of the bed while Paul swaddled him tightly in his blanket like a cocoon.

"Thanks, Dad. You obviously haven't lost your magic touch."

Tom laughed and went back into the kitchen where Rose was busy putting teacups and saucers on a tray ready to carry out to the living room. Jessica still looked confrontational and so Tom went over and gave her a quick hug. "You know something Jess, your mother and I really miss you and Rob. It's not the same as when you lived in London; Montreal is definitely a long haul away and your mother and I are not getting any younger. Somehow the drive takes its toll out on both of us. I hope that you're happy living there."

Jessica looked miserable, in a small voice she said, "Oh, Dad, I miss seeing Mom and you so much, but Rob is so much happier, and I actually really like Montreal."

"Well, love, as long as you're all happy, that's all that counts."

They could hear Abby and Ella shrieking with laughter as their Uncle Paul chased them around the living room. Jessica rolled her eyes and muttered something about her brother not growing up. Rose carried in the tray of tea and called the family together. A quick cup of tea and Jessica, Abby, and Ella would be on the road to Toronto and Paul and Atsuko would also soon hit the road, finally leaving Tom and Rose in glorious peace again.

TWENTY-THREE

The team had gathered and John, after he had made his phone call to Rose, hurried back to join them in The Lion's Hall.

"Right, good afternoon everyone. The biggest news is that Rose Blair's sister's car has been found, and the bad news is that another car has been stolen outside the Clinton Slots; it was taken from the same car park where we found Kate's car. We now have an APB alert out on a pale blue Toyota Corolla, registration number YGH 675.

Constable Ryan, anything further on our stolen art theft theory?"

Constable Ryan opened her laptop and pulled up her notes. She began to read directly from them, "In 1997 The Rijks Museum commissioned Van Heuzen Art Restorers to clean and restore two of their Old Dutch master's paintings, *The Milkmaid* and *The Girl with a Pearl Earring*. The museum had used Van Heuzen many times before and had no cause for alarm, which of course, in hindsight, they should have, because our good friend Karel de Vries and his partner

Gerrit Van Heuzen were part of the scam. Gert, one of Karel's cousins, was an expert painter, his forgeries were identical to the originals, so much so that Sotheby's could never detect the forgery. Now, guv, here's the interesting part. A Vermeer painting, *The Milkmaid*, recently came under scrutiny at The Rijks Museum by one of their employed art specialists who claimed that the painting was a forgery. It was something to do with the age of the canvas which alerted the woman." Here Holly checked her notes, "A Dr. Moleevaar, was adamant that *The Milkmaid* was a reproduction, albeit a very cleverly executed one, and this caused a big uproar in the museum as Sotheby's had already authenticated the piece and had refused to back down on their word. I checked into the records and found that this same painting had been sent for a 'clean-up' to Van Heuzen's a few weeks before our two men, Karel and Gerrit came to Canada. This was twenty-two years ago."

DCI Hargreaves and the rest of the team were silent as they absorbed the information and possible implications for the investigation. Finally John spoke, "So, we possibly have a stolen Vermeer painting stashed away in a fishing rod case. Any idea what this painting is worth?

Constable Ryan answered straight away, "Yes, guv, remember, I told you that in 2010 a Vermeer sold at auction for forty million dollars.

"That's motivation enough for murder," Sergeant Flowers muttered under his breath.

DCI Hargreaves glanced at him before speaking, "The trouble with all of this is that it's all pure circumstantial evidence and pure conjecture. We have no proof that there is actually a stolen painting rolled up and hidden in the fishing rod case, no proof of anything other than the murder. I do, however, have a report from Interpol, finally, outlining Gerrit

Van Heuzen's background. Much of what you have so dili-
gently researched, Constable Ryan, corroborates this; Van
Heuzen did have a business restoring old paintings and yes,
Karel de Vries was employed by him. Both men were charged
with grand theft and forgery in 1997 after a Vermeer was identified as a very good forgery and reproduction of the original,
but we have absolutely no proof that a Vermeer was stolen in
1997 let alone the painting finding it's way to Bayfield, and
Windmill Lake Eco Park specifically." John sighed deeply and
continued to talk, trying very hard not to show his frustration
to the team. "No, we have to continue to treat this as a murder
investigation and not get too sidetracked by the art theft
possibility."

He glanced at Constable Ryan who looked suitably
crushed. John continued, feeling bad that he had hurt the one
officer who had provided the team with the most information.
He continued with a softer voice, "I do have the pathologists
report and it appears that the deceased was not a well man. He
apparently was living off borrowed time with a massive
tumour in his stomach which, had he not been so brutally
murdered, would probably have taken his life soon enough.
John paused and pulled up the notes that he had been given
before continuing his report.

"According to ballistics, a 0.8 Luger was used to kill him,
an older version of the modern Luger which makes me think
that the gun had been stashed along with the fishing rod case,
but once again, that is just pure conjecture."

He put his notes down and looked at his team in earnest.

"No, team, we need to concentrate on tracking down Karel
de Vries. We now know that he was last located at the Clinton
Slots because that is where Rose Blair's sister's car was abandoned. It is imperative that we track down the pale blue

Corolla which was stolen from that car park; find the car and we just might find the man or at least know in which direction he is headed. Constables Elliot and Brown, I want you to circulate photographs of both Karel de Vries and the Corolla in and around The Slots. Someone will have seen him I am sure. Sergeant, I want you to interview Kate once again. She was the last person to have seen him before he left the Bayfield area. I am going to talk to the Blairs again and then, I'm afraid it is up to the public to give us any further leads.

John stood up and prepared to go before reasserting, "This case is rapidly going lukewarm on us before it has even started. I am afraid it will go stone cold if we don't get a break soon. Go to it all of you and bring us back some results."

The team shuffled miserably out of The Lion's Hall, a light sense of desperation hovering like a bad smell around them. Nobody ever wanted an investigation to go cold, certainly not DCI Hargreaves who was still out to prove himself with this being his first murder case in Canada.

TWENTY-FOUR

Rose made Tom and her breakfast of poached eggs on toast and placed the plate in front of her husband who was agitated as he was already running late for his game of golf. She had dinner to prepare for their guest, DCI Hargreaves, that night. Maybe she should invite Kate, she thought as she cleared away the breakfast plates and pulled out her mixing bowl preparing to make a ginger pudding.

Kate, who had still been brooding heavily since the previous day, was relieved to hear her sister's voice on the telephone.

"Do you fancy coming around for dinner tonight, Kate?" Rose asked.

"Oh, what time? I'm out this afternoon and probably won't return much before five-thirty?"

"Where are you going? Is it your turn at the shelter?"

"No, it's my Red Hat get together. We're going to Blyth Theatre to a matinee and I've already paid otherwise I would cancel, but I should be back in Bayfield certainly no later than six o'clock."

"Oh, well that will do just fine. DCI Hargreaves isn't coming until six and we won't eat much before seven. Great, see you then. Hey, sis, enjoy the show."

Rose put the phone down and busied herself with creaming the butter and sugar together before adding in some flour, ginger, and eggs. She would serve the pudding with some hot custard as Rose knew that Brits liked their puddings with custard. The main course would also be suitably English with a steak and Guinness pie, mashed potatoes, cauliflower au gratin, and green beans from their garden. *But what should I make as an appetizer?* Rose thought while mentally going through a few alternatives. *Maybe smoked salmon on rye bread or bruschetta or melon with thin slices of ham.* In the end, she settled on a Mediterranean sardine pate to be served with fingers of hot toast. *Right,* Rose thought, *Tom can organize the drinks.* With that in mind she was about to make herself a cup of coffee when the phone rang. It was Anne, their daughter from Halifax.

"Hi, Mom, I've got some really big news."

Anne was their drama queen as there was always something happening in her life. In fact, Rose had only commented to Tom the other day that everything had appeared to be ominously quiet on that front. "Go on then, darling, spill the beans." Rose said.

"I've been offered a head of department position at Ryerson in Toronto."

Rose could tell by her daughter's voice that she was hugely excited.

"That's great news, but what about Greg? What about his job?"

Anne and Greg were both professors at Dalhousie University in Halifax. Greg had been head of the Astro-Physics department for five years and Rose really could not see him relinquishing his position for a move to Toronto.

"Oh, Greg says that he's ready to retire and be a stay at home dad."

They had two adorable children whom Rose and Tom only got to see once a year. Their names were Oliver and Amelia. Moving to Toronto would certainly bring them closer, but Rose had her doubts.

"Well, my darling, congratulations, that's great news. I suppose they want you to start in September?"

"Yes, but Greg says that I should go on ahead and he'll deal with the house."

Rose was quite shocked, "You mean you're going to sell your lovely house? What about the children? They love that house."

"Well, Mom, I was going to ask if dad and you could look after Ollie and Amelia just for a couple of weeks while we get ourselves sorted? I'm not sure if we're going to rent or buy in Toronto. There's so much to think about; I'm actually feeling a bit overwhelmed right now."

Rose could hear the slight wobble in her daughter's voice and so she answered gently,

"Umm...well, I suppose we could have the kids for a couple of weeks, but will they be alright with us?"

Rose's heart sank at the thought of looking after the children as Oliver was such an energetic little boy and Amelia was still learning to walk and talk and seemed awfully young to be left. She tentatively asked "Umm... when exactly were you thinking we would have them stay?"

"Oh, we were thinking about the first two weeks in August if that's okay by you?"

Gosh, Rose thought, *only two weeks away*. But she said, "I'll talk to your dad, darling, and let you know tomorrow, but I'm sure that it will be alright."

They talked a little longer and then Rose said that she was in the middle of cooking and she had to get on with it. As she put the phone down Rose sighed thinking, two whole weeks of their grandchildren, *that's enough to finish me off*, she thought and felt suddenly quite exhausted at the mere thought of baby sitting her grandchildren.

TWENTY-FIVE

Kate decided that enough was enough. She would quit feeling sorry for herself and enjoy the day ahead of her. Since moving to Bayfield she had joined The Red Hat Ladies and had found instant companionship with the rest of the women. Putting on her finest attire, she donned a purple and red wide brimmed hat and looked at herself in the mirror.

"You look alright, Miss Katie," she said out loud deliberately blocking out the image of Karel caressing her body and pretty well whispering the same words. "I am a survivor," she said again out loud and this time much louder and then she proceeded to walk tall and close the front door and stride out to her car.

Thirty minutes later she was parked in the car park at the front of the supermarket in Blyth with half an hour to spare before the show started. Kate decided to go window shopping to kill the time and although Blyth was only a small town, there were a number of really good shops to browse. Of course, in the summer months the normally sleepy little town became crazy busy with bus loads of tourists coming to the theatre which put on at least six plays a year, all written by Canadian authors. The Red Hatters, all twenty of them, had booked seats to see a show. Some of the women had met for lunch at The Queens Bakery across the road from the theatre, but Kate had chosen to abstain as she knew that Rose would be cooking up a storm for that evening's dinner.

Walking past The Queen's Bakery she waved to her friends and continued past Part 2 Bistro and to the corner of the road to where The Blyth Inn stood. She was about to walk past and cross the road when she happened to glance through the window into what presumably was a small dining room. There sitting at a round table, eating what looked like a pizza, was none other than Karel de Vries. Kate stood rooted to the sidewalk, her jaw dropped and a small cry emitted from her mouth and then she ran as fast as she could back to her car. Had he seen her? She didn't think so, but her heart was beating so fast she could barely think, let alone breath. *Where's my phone?* Kate thought and then she remembered that she had left it at home fearful in case it rang during the performance.

She got out of her car and walked across the road to the theatre where she asked the box office if she could use their phone. Kate placed her call to Rose who assured her that she would contact DCI Hargreaves straight away but suggested that in the meantime Kate should enjoy the show as she would be safe amongst the crowds of people.

Back in the pizza bar of The Blyth Inn, Karel quietly fumed as he thought to himself, *what was that bitch doing in Blyth?* Now that she had seen him that meant that his cover was blown and he would have to move quickly before the cops would be onto him.

"Potverdore!" he exclaimed, "damn, damn, damn!" he reached for his phone and texted Annek.

On the move again, heading for Goderich.

He would be far more anonymous in a bigger town and this time he would check into an Airbnb which again would be easier to hide from the public eye. With that settled, Karel went back to his room and checked out leaving by the back door. Of course he would have to ditch the car again which meant finding another car with the keys left in the ignition which Karel knew wouldn't be particularly challenging as Canadians seemed to be far too trustworthy, either that or just plain foolish. He found a small Ford Focus parked on the side street at the corner of the Inn and soon he was on the road again once again driving past the spectacular brewery, Cowbell, and on through Londesborough and into Clinton where he turned right onto Highway 8 and began his final journey into Goderich. The Airbnb he had booked was close to The Square in the centre of the town. He planned to leave the stolen car on a street near enough so that he could walk to his destination. Once there and checked in he would text Anneka to let her know his address and with a bit of luck she might be arriving very soon.

DCI Hargreaves was just finishing off his pint and burger at The Albion when his phone rang. It was Rose Blair sounding distinctly agitated. Her sister had just seen Karel, presumably the murderer, inside The Blyth Inn and was naturally quite freaked out and wanted the police to go there immediately. John looked at his watch, 1:45 p.m., and the team meeting would be starting in just fifteen minutes. He would send Constable Ryan and Elliot to check out The Blyth Inn and to speak to Kate. He called the officers and sent them on their way, then he walked over to The Lion's Hall, and opened up his laptop.

There in his inbox he found two interesting letters. One was from a Dr. Moleevaar, a leading forensic art specialist from the Rijks in Amsterdam. She had heard that enquiries had been made regarding the Vermeer painting, *The Milkmaid*. The old Dutch Masters were her specialty and, indeed, the painting in question had haunted her for over twenty years. Although Sotheby's had in 2010 conducted a thorough appraisal of the painting currently hanging on a wall in the museum and had concluded that it was indeed an authentic Vermeer, Dr. Moleevaar had, even then, her doubts.

She had recently conducted her own tests on the fabric that the painting had been painted on, using a few threads from the edge of the canvas. She had managed to have them analysed under a microscope. The linen used to make the canvas in question, was made from cotton with a GMO stamp which most certainly was not from the 17th century where they had used hemp to make their canvass. The Rijks Museum had been totally shocked by this discovery and, in order to play down the fall out of bad publicity, they had begged the doctor to keep the news of the forgery to herself. In the meantime, efforts were doubled to track down the original *Milkmaid* and so, when word had got out that the painting might possibly be in Canada, she had been asked to go and check it out. According to Dr. Moleevaar's email, she would be arriving the following day and would like to meet the officer in charge of the investigation.

John re-read the email several times. The trouble was they had no solid proof that there ever had been a painting stashed inside the fishing-rod case; there was only Kate's word that she had felt something rolled up, possibly a canvas, inside the case.

Whilst John did not mind meeting up with the art specialist, he couldn't help but think that she had been sent on some sort of wild goose chase.

The second email confirmed what Constable Ryan had already researched that the deceased, Gerrit Van Heuzen, age 54, had indeed owned and operated an art restoring business up until 1996 when he was caught trying to sell a Vermeer to a dealer in Michigan. Karel and Gerrit had been put away for twenty years.

Right, John thought to himself, *it was time to chart everything on the white board.* Under sub-titles of people, places, and objects, he wrote out everything that the team knew about the case. In the end, when seeing everything written out, it really looked like the team had achieved quite a lot. What the board could not reveal was that Karel was proving to be quite the slippery customer. He hoped that Constable's Ryan and Elliot would strike lucky and sniff out a trail which might lead them to their murderer, but he wouldn't hold his breath.

Kate had waited in the theatre foyer and so had missed the first half of the hilarious show. Finally two officers appeared and took her statement and then she was able to creep into the auditorium and join the rest of the Red Hatters. In the meantime, Constable Ryan and Elliot walked across the road to The Blyth Inn where they interviewed the landlord.

"Ah, you just missed the man by about twenty minutes. He checked out in a bit of a hurry. He was a fisherman by the looks of things. No, he barely said two words to me."

"Did he say where he was going?" Constable Ryan asked.

"No, he just wanted to settle up with cash, which I have to say, is unusual these days."

"You said that his name was Gert Dupuis? Was he Dutch?"

"Well, he spoke perfect English, but now you mention it, he did have quite a strong accent."

"Okay, did you notice what car he was driving?" Constable Elliot asked.

"Yes, it was a pale blue Corolla. He parked it behind the Inn in the car park reserved for guests."

"Right, thank you." Constable Ryan said and the two officers left the reception area to go and check out the rear car park. Sure enough the Corolla was parked neatly at the back of the piece of land used by The Blyth Inn. Constable Ryan pulled out her phone and called DCI Hargreaves.

"Hi, guv, it looks like he's done a runner on us. The stolen car is parked behind the Inn. I suspect that he's taken another car, but quite where he's gone, that's anyone's guess."

Meanwhile back in Bayfield, John put away his phone and let out a deep groan and turned to the rest of the team who had begun to wear looks of despondency on their young faces. "Okay, let's go through our notes from the beginning and see if we're missing something."

TWENTY-SIX

The ginger pudding turned out a treat and it had even kept its shape when Rose had turned it out onto a serving platter. She would zip it into the microwave oven just to warm it through before serving it for dessert that evening. The steak and Guinness pie was ready to bake in the oven, the cauliflower au gratin prepared, potatoes peeled, and the sardine pâté chilling in the fridge and it was still only 4:30 p.m. Rose was ahead of herself and so there was time enough for her to take a short break, change into something a bit smarter than her jeans and sweatshirt, and maybe Tom would take the dogs for a quick walk before their guests arrived for dinner. Rose walked to their bedroom and found Tom lying down. She was quite alarmed as he never lay down in the daytime and, come to think of it, he had come in from his game of golf and not said a single word to her and had quietly gone off to their bedroom to lie down. "Tom, darling, are you feeling alright?"

Tom opened his eyes and nodded his head slowly, "Umm... I'm okay, love, just feeling incredibly tired and my shoulder aches a bit. That game of golf with Doug just knocked the stuffing out of me. I'll just rest for a while. What time are we expecting our guests?"

"Oh, not for another couple of hours yet. Do you have any pain or dizziness, Tom?"

Tom said no and then closed his eyes. Rose looked at him with concern, worry lines etched into her face. "I'll wake you up in time for dinner, darling," With that she quickly changed her clothes, brushed her hair, and grabbed the two dog leashes hanging up by the front door. Ben and Puff rushed over. "Walkies you two."

Walking was always a good time for Rose to think, whereas baking was her therapy time to relax. She found physically getting out of the house and removing herself from all the distractions that it offered her free reign to really think. *Poor Kate*, her thoughts immediately jumped to the shock of being nearly drowned and then seeing the man again in Blyth must have been truly scary for her. What was she to do about her sister, Rose thought. It was a real shame that their mutual friend, Linda, had been away so much as they had hit it off so well together that previous summer. She had tried to encourage Kate to join the Croquet Club as that was a great place to meet people, but no, her sister had said that it was not for her. Then she had also turned down going out to fitness classes but had instead decided to volunteer her time at the animal rescue in Goderich. What her sister really needed to do was to get a good friend in her life, a companion, male or female, Rose thought.

She walked down Bayfield Terrace to Pioneer Park and then walked down the wooden steps to the beach. Although it was a beautiful afternoon, the beach was almost deserted except for one lone kayaker bobbing up and down in his small kayak. Rose let the dogs off their leashes and they made a beeline for the lake.

She continued to walk towards the pier where she could see three fishermen sitting on little fold-up stools, their rods in hand and lines in the water. Seeing them made Rose think about the murderer, Karel de Vries and his fishing rod case. She wondered once more what it was that was rolled up inside. Kate had said that it was some sort of fabric or canvas, but she hadn't had enough time to look properly before Karel had entered the room. Maybe DCI Hargreaves might be able to shed some more light on the contents of the case. It had been four days since the murder and seemingly not much progress on apprehending the murderer. Rose knew from all the years of friendship with DCI Susan Parker, John's predecessor, that cases could go cold, not all were easily solved, and many were left on the shelf unsolved and seemingly unsolvable. She hoped that DCI Hargreaves succeeded in closing the case as he seemed somehow more vulnerable than other police officers Rose had known. Maybe it was because he was British and still a bit of an enigma, plus the fact that his eyes looked so lost and sad. Rose hoped that after the evening's dinner she might get to know DCI Hargreaves a bit more.

TWENTY-SEVEN

K arel paced up and down like a captured lion anxiously waiting for the arrival of his dearest friend, Anneka. She had texted him to say she was a mere half an hour away and he had returned her text with the address of the Airbnb that he had booked. When he had registered with Airbnb, he had to give two pieces of I.D. and unfortunately he had to use his real name for this purpose as his driving license and credit card were the only form of I.D. available for him to use. It didn't really matter as Anneka and he would be well gone before the police could track him to the Airbnb. The Ford Focus had been ditched and that too would be found pretty quickly, but also, by then he would be away with Anneka, in fact, as soon as she arrived, he wanted to pack his rucksack and clear out.

Although he had known her for what seemed like a lifetime, and indeed he had known her since primary school, it had only been since his release from prison that he had got to know her on an intimate level. Twenty-two years ago Anneka had been a graduate and in the interim period of his incarceration, her career had blossomed. She was known to be one of the world's leading specialists on the old Dutch Masters. She alone, other than Gerrit Van Heuzen, and he didn't count anymore because he was dead, she was the only person who knew about the stolen Vermeer.

Karel glanced outside from his upstairs window scanning the road. Anneka would have rented a car from the airport, but he wasn't sure what car she would be driving. He had told her that the owners of the Airbnb were expecting her as he had informed them that his partner would be arriving later that evening. They, themselves, were going out so he would have the house to himself until they got back later that night. *Good,* Karel had thought, *Anneka loved a bit of rough play;* they would be able to make as much noise as they liked.

Finally, a red Chevrolet pulled up into the driveway and there she stood, the girl of his dreams, his pocketbook lover, all five feet of her with her mane of red gold hair and elfin-like features. He ran downstairs to meet her embracing her in a huge hug as he drew her into the hall and led her upstairs to his bedroom.

"God, Anneka, it's been too long!"

She looked at him and laughed, "Sure, babe, it's been all of one week, now come to mama, come..." She pulled off her light summer dress in one quick, fluid movement and kicked off her high heeled shoes. She wore no underwear and immediately Karel was aroused by her stunning naked body fairly glowing under the bedside light.

They made passionate love with complete abandon after which they both lay spent side by side on the bed totally satiated. After a while Anneka reached over and stroked Karel's face with her fingertips saying softly, "Babe, show me the Vermeer."

Karel got out of bed and reached over to the fishing rod case which lay on the floor by his rucksack. He unzipped the canister and gently, almost reverently, pulled out the rolled-up canvas. Slowly he unrolled the painting and held it up high for Anneka to see.

With huge eyes almost crying with sheer awe and delight, Anneka viewed *The Milkmaid* in all its detail. It was such a simple composition made up of a rather plain looking woman pouring milk from a terracotta jug into a bowl which sat on a blue table clothed table beside a basket of rustic looking bread. The woman wore a basic frock with a blue apron tied around her waist and a white cap upon her head. Vermeer had painted only thirty-five paintings in total and nearly all of them had depicted intimate everyday activities. *The Milkmaid* was sometimes called *The Kitchen Maid,* and it was actually painted in 1658 when the artist was just twenty-six years old. Vermeer only lived a comparatively short life dying at the age of forty-three in 1675. His paintings sold for millions and at the last valuation, *The Milkmaid* was valued at forty million dollars.

"You actually succeeded, babe. We're going to be rich. Now come to mama, come, I'm going to show you how grateful I am."

Anneka pushed Karel down onto the bed firstly taking the painting from him and rolling it back up to slip it back into the fishing-rod case. She then proceeded to sit astride him. Their love making was so intense that they did not hear the Airbnb hosts return.

Karel lay sleeping snoring gently as Anneka crept out of bed and quietly got dressed. She opened her carrier bag and pulled out a silk scarf and two long plastic zip ties. She approached the bed and quickly grabbed Karel's hands and, using the zip ties, she tied them together. Karel's eyes flashed open as his mouth started to form the words, "Potverdore!"

"Just a little game, babe, shh... you don't want to disturb the neighbours."

She grabbed the silk scarf and tied it over his mouth and then zipped his ankles together. All this time Karel had lain on the bed prone anticipating some kinky sex that Anneka had dreamt up, so that when she pulled out a plastic bag and started to put it over his head, he suddenly began to feel panicky. She pulled the sides of the bag together and looked at her watch. Just a few more minutes and he would be dead.

TWENTY-EIGHT

DCI Hargreaves and Rose's sister, Kate, arrived within minutes of each other, both carrying bottles of wine. John was just explaining to Rose how strange he had found it having to go to the LCBO to buy wine where back in England he could have bought it at their local supermarket. When Kate appeared, he immediately asked how she was feeling having seen Karel lurking in the shadows in Blyth.

Kate had been determined to put it all behind her and just laughed saying, "Oh, I really don't want to ever see that man again, but, you know, the play was really good."

They had all gone to sit in the sunroom and Rose brought out the pâté while Tom saw to everyone's drinks.

Rose made a toast, "To you, John. Welcome to Bayfield."

And then Kate asked him where he had lived before.

John answered hesitantly to begin with saying, "Oh, I'm originally from Zambia. In fact, my family still lives there, in Kitwe where I was raised. I went to university in London, England and got my first job in the police force working for the

Met. The past twenty years I've worked for the Bristol Serious Crimes Squad and now I've been with the London unit for barely two months."

Undeterred Kate ploughed on with her questions, "But what brought you to Canada?"

John went quiet for a while before answering, "My wife died five years ago and our only child, Rachael, married a Canadian. They moved to London, Ontario and had a baby, my grandson, just one year ago. I wanted to be closer to my daughter and wanted to be a proper grandpa to Liam. I retired a couple of years ago and had absolutely no intention of ever working again, but this position with Serious Crimes in London became available and they were pretty desperate to fill it. So here I am, trying to solve one hell of a difficult murder and feeling frustrated by the current impasse."

Rose interrupted the conversation by calling out from the kitchen, "Right, would you all like to come to the table, dinner is ready."

The ale pie was delicious and the ginger pudding and custard was much appreciated by John. They were about to adjoin to the living room when John's phone rang. It was the Goderich dispatch. There had been an attempted murder on one Karel de Vries.

After John left rather quickly, Kate took her leave too, leaving Rose and Tom to clear away the dinner things and generally tidy up. All of a sudden Tom grabbed the kitchen sink saying, "I don't feel too good, love. I think that you need to take me to the hospital."

Rose looked at him alarmed at the pastiness of his face. He had a thin film of perspiration running across his brow. She grabbed the car keys and shouldering Tom the best she could, they both stumbled out to the car. Rose drove like a maniac while Tom lay on the back seat barely moving. "Hold on, darling," she said.

They reached Goderich in record time and were just approaching the junction with Britannia Road and the highway when a bright red Chevrolet came careering out of seemingly nowhere and smashed into the rear side of Rose's Volvo. Rose leapt out of the car just in time to see a woman with a mane of long, red hair reverse and swerve around the car and then drive off like a bat out of hell down the highway towards Bayfield. Rose looked at the dent in her car and then jumped back in and continued on to the hospital where she parked at the back by the emergency and ran inside shouting for help. Two paramedics ran out with a stretcher and within minutes Tom was being wheeled inside leaving Rose in a state of anxiety.

"What do I do, what do I do?" Rose muttered to no one in particular while pacing up and down the corridor of the hospital. A kindly nurse approached her with a clip board and suggested that they sit down while she asked Rose some questions.

Halfway through the questions Rose saw Tom being wheeled out into the hallway. She got up to follow him, but was quickly restrained by the nurse, who said, "Mrs. Blair, just wait, your husband is undergoing some vital tests. We think that he's had a heart attack, but we won't know for sure until he's had an angiogram."

The waiting was interminable, but finally they wheeled Tom back down the hallway and this time Rose was allowed to follow them into a ward where they carefully tucked him into a bed and hooked him up to a machine which showed his heart beats. She sat on the bedside chair and took hold of Tom's hand. Two years ago she had been the one in intensive care being comforted by Tom. It was funny how life had come full circle and now Rose knew exactly what anguish Tom had been faced with then.

"Tom, my darling, I love you. Be strong, my love, be strong." She whispered and kissed him tenderly. He had been sedated and so she was not certain if he had heard her or not. She squeezed his hand and let out a deep sigh. Somehow the thought of life without Tom seemed unbearable. She rested her head on his shoulder and softly cried saying, "Hold on, Tom, hold on."

TWENTY-NINE

DCI Hargreaves arrived at the scene of the crime just as the paramedics were loading up the stretcher. One of them turned to him as he closed the ambulance door and said, "He's alive, but just barely." And they were off, lights blazing and sirens blaring headed for The Alexander Marine Hospital.

John went into the house which was a substantial 1940s arts and craft building with a wide covered veranda embracing two sides of the building. A couple in their sixties stood in the hallway looking rather forlorn as they watched the ambulance pull away. John introduced himself quickly and asked if he could have a word with them. He followed them into a charming living room immaculately decorated in pale pastels with a white sofa and matching love seat.

"Please, officer, take a seat. May I get you a drink?" the man of the house politely asked.

John was well aware that he was probably over the limit already having come straight from Rose and Tom Blair's dinner party and so he declined saying, "No, thank you, but I really do need to know what happened here tonight."

The woman looked very tired and a trifle nervous, hesitating before she spoke softly with what John detected to be a slight Glaswegian accent.

"Well, you see officer, we run a wee Airbnb business, just the one room and that poor man had just checked in today and told us that his partner would be joining him later. Alan and I were going out and so we left him here alone. When we returned there was a red car parked in the driveway which we presumed belonged to his partner. It was only nine o'clock, but we do tend to go to bed quite early and Alan and I were just setting up the table for breakfast next day when we heard," here she paused, her cheeks turning a bright red as she looked to her husband to continue.

Alan took up the tale, "Umm... there is no other way of telling it, the couple was at it like a pair of rutting deer, lots of grunts, bumps, and squeals of delight," the man coughed and continued, "anyway, all went quiet so Betty and I locked up and were about to go to bed when we heard a bit of a commotion, followed by a bump as if something heavy had hit the floor. Then we heard the front door open and close and I looked out of the window and saw a woman drive away in the red car. Betty was worried about the loud thud that we had heard and so we opened the guest bedroom door, and I'm so glad we did, because there the poor man was tied up with a plastic bag over his head. He was barely breathing and in a right state."

John asked if he could see the room and the first thing that he noticed was the fishing rod case, the zip was open and the lid hung over the side of the case. John quickly looked inside and sure enough there was a canvas rolled up. It looked as if he had not only found the murderer, Karel, but had called up trumps with finding the famous painting, if indeed it was the stolen Vermeer hidden inside. He left Alan and Betty taking the fishing rod case with him feeling very elated indeed.

THIRTY

Tom opened his eyes and looked up to see his beloved Rose her face creased with worry and lined with fatigue.

"Ah love don't look so concerned. I'm going to be fine I promise."

"Oh, Tom, you gave me such a fright. Look, they're taking you to London first thing in the morning and you're going to have a stent put in; something about a blocked valve. I'm sure the doctor will explain it all to you. Anyhow, they want you to sleep and so I'm going home. I'll see you tomorrow at St. Joseph's Hospital in London."

Tom looked at Rose through sleepy eyes and whispered, "I love you, Rose." Which made her feel all weepy again.

She squeezed his hand and bent over to kiss him tenderly. "I love you too, my darling." And she quietly left the room trying very hard not to cry.

When Rose arrived home, she suddenly remembered the car accident. She had been so focused on getting Tom to the hospital that she had dismissed the whole incident as trivial.

Now she looked at the damage and sighed deeply. There was a definite dent in the rear left wing, but at least the bumper had not been damaged. Her Volvo was twelve years old and quite battered, maybe another dent would go unnoticed.

Ben and Puff greeted her excitedly. *You would think that I had been away weeks*, Rose thought as she let them out into the garden and surveyed the pristine kitchen. Kate must have stayed on and, judging by the tidy kitchen and dining table, she must have cleaned everything up and put all the plates away. Rose found her sister curled up on the sofa sound asleep with the television still on. She was just tiptoeing out of the room when Kate opened her eyes and said, "Is that you, Rose? How's Tom?"

The following hour was spent just talking over several pots of tea, until finally, the sisters both called it a day with Rose saying, "You might as well stay here, Kate."

She agreed saying, "Oh, and Rose, I'm coming with you to London tomorrow, no ifs or buts about it!"

They hugged each other and went off to bed too tired to talk anymore. It was one thirty in the morning.

THIRTY-ONE

DCI Hargreaves woke up with a jolt and looked at his watch. It was already eight o'clock, his team would be assembled by nine and he had a report to write and summarize the previous nights turn up for the books. In his mind he had been going through the strange twist that the case had taken with the attempted murder of their prime suspect, Karel de Vries. The doctors at the hospital had said that he would be fine just bruised from the fall from the bed to the floor which had of course saved him from ultimate suffocation.

They would be interrogating him later on that day after the team had been put in the picture. John checked his emails and muttered an expletive. He had completely forgotten about Dr. Moleevaar who had said that she would be at The Lion's Hall around nine that morning. *Well at least I'll have something to show her*, he thought while cyeing the fishing rod case now propped up against the bedroom wardrobe. John had felt thoroughly elated last night after they had found Karel de Vries, but now in the cool light of the day he felt somewhat deflated and something still didn't sit right with him. He did not have the luxury of time to dwell on matters as breakfast called and then he would have to hot foot it along to The Lion's Hall if he was to get there in time. Grabbing the black fishing rod case, John made his way downstairs and walked into the Willow Room ready to grab a coffee and croissant. The dining room was busy with the two waitresses worked off their feet. He decided to forego breakfast altogether and maybe grab a coffee to go from Shop Bike and join the rest of his team.

Arriving at The Lion's Hall with ten minutes to spare, John flicked back through his case notes reading the limited amount of evidence they had accumulated, which was mostly circumstantial. He couldn't help but feel that everything hinged on the fishing rod case which at that moment sat propped up against the wall. John walked over and picked it up, unzipped the top, and gently pulled out the rolled-up canvas. Very slowly he unrolled it and for the first time set his eyes on *The Milkmaid*. The painting was beautifully executed as far as John's untrained eyes could see, but the subject matter was rather mundane. If Constable Ryan's research had been accurate, he was looking at something worth somewhere between thirty to forty million dollars and that felt insane. He was just in the middle of rolling up the canvas when Sergeant Flowers, followed by the rest of the team, ambled in.

"Have you got what I think you have, sir?" Sergeant Flowers said with some excitement in his voice. John nodded and proceeded to tell the team the whole story from the previous night's encounter.

"So you see, we've got our man and even retrieved the famous Vermeer. But I keep asking myself why don't I feel excited?"

Constable Ryan interjected, "Maybe it's because it all seems to have been tied up so easily; almost handed to us on a plate, so to speak."

"Yes, that's exactly what I think I feel. Anyway, we'll hear the whole story when we bring him in for questioning this afternoon. Right now he's recuperating in the hospital. I've got an officer on duty outside his bedroom door so he won't be going anywhere in a hurry. Very soon I'm expecting our visitor from the Rijks Museum, Dr. Moleevaar to turn up. We at least can show her the painting and she will hopefully be able to authenticate it one way or another."

As if right on cue, there was a knock on the door and a petite, elfin looking woman with a flaming mane of red hair stepped into the room.

"Am I in the right place? I'm looking for DCI Harg-reaves?" she said with a slightly husky voice.

John smiled and extended his hand, "You must be Dr. Moleevaar, pleased to meet you and this is my team. We were just discussing the painting that we found rolled up in this fishing rod case. I'm sure that you can't wait to see it yourself!"

Anneka nodded enthusiastically and helped John pull the canvas out. She held her breath as they unrolled the painting and then she scanned the picture with her camera before turning it over.

"Look here, DCI Hargreaves, look at the old canvas. You can almost see the individual threads woven together to make the cloth. I will have to run this through our spectrometer and get the threads tested to see if they are GMO, but at first glance it looks like the real thing."

Constable Ryan could barely contain herself and she blurted out rather abruptly, "You mean, doctor, like genetically modified corn and wheat?"

Dr. Moleevaar nodded saying, "Yes, exactly. For the past thirty odd years farmers have used GMO crops almost exclusively from corn, flax, or cotton. Canvas is traditionally made from hemp which is grown abundantly in our country. Modern day canvases are made with GMO cotton or flax usually from the States, whereas three hundred years ago when this painting was painted, the canvas would have been made from coarse linen locally grown and certainly not from a GMO plant. We do know that Vermeer had all of his canvass made for him and the artisans making the canvases grew their own crop to weave into cloth. A simple test can prove its origin and settle the dispute one way or another."

Once again Constable Ryan interrupted Dr. Moleevaar by saying, "I read that *The Milkmaid* currently hanging in the Rijks Museum was actually authenticated by Sotheby's in 2011. Did they conduct a canvas test then?"

"They took some paint samples and x-rayed the painting. It really has only been in the last five years that we have been able to test the thread for GMO's. The painting in 2011 passed the legitimate paint test and the x-ray showed no other painting beneath and so Sotheby's concluded that it was indeed the original Vermeer. My doctorate was on the Old Dutch Masters with particular emphasis on Vermeer's work. I have long thought that *The Milkmaid* was a forgery. Today I feel that I have been vindicated and I thank you. Now, I must leave you to your work as I have a plane to catch in four hours and a very precious cargo to accompany me."

Anneka carefully rolled the canvas up and gently pushed it back into the fishing rod case.

"This is the perfect case to transport the canvas. I once again thank you for finding the stolen Vermeer. As soon as all the tests have been conducted, I will notify you of the results. The museum will be officially contacting you too."

She looked at her watch and with a quick flick of her mane of red hair she turned and left The Lion's Hall.

There was a shocked silence in the room as the team took in what had just taken place. John was the first one to break the stunned silence,

"We've just handed over a forty million dollar painting to someone we don't even know. I hope Constable Ryan that your search verified Dr. Moleevaar's qualifications?"

Holly looked pale but she answered clearly and confidently, "Yes, guv, her credentials all add up, and I did take the added precaution of contacting the Director of the Rijks Museum and he assured me that Dr. Moleevaar was the best in the field. I think that she's okay, guv."

"Thank you, Constable, let's hope so otherwise we're in deep you know what!"

THIRTY-TWO

Rose woke up feeling disorientated and groggy. She could hear her sister gently snoring in the guest bedroom. Looking at her watch she decided it was time to call the hospital and see how Tom was after a night's sedation. The ward sister spoke to Rose and told her that Tom had woken feeling much better and that everything was on schedule. The ambulance would drive him to London where his surgery was booked for noon. They would be leaving Goderich around eight thirty.

Rose thanked the nurse and glanced at her watch again. Before she put the phone down, she said, "Do you think that you could tell Tom that I'll be at the hospital in London waiting for him and tell him I love him."

As she said those three words Rose choked up and quickly put the phone down.

Kate had obviously heard her talking as she appeared in the doorway looking decidedly sleepy.

"Good morning, Kate, do you want a cup of tea?"

Rose didn't wait for a reply and Kate meekly followed her

into the kitchen like a puppy dog. Puff and Ben made a beeline for the back door. Once again checking the time Rose decided that after their tea, she would take the dogs for a quick walk. It was only seven forty-five but she really wanted to be on the road no later than nine.

Looking at her sleepy sister, Rose said, "Kate, you really don't have to come with me. Why don't you go back to bed?"

"Of course I'm coming with you. Look, I'll be alright once I've had my tea and maybe some breakfast."

"Are you sure?" Rose asked gently.

"Of course I'm sure. We're family and families stick together in times of emergency."

"Okay, then I am going to go and get dressed and then take the dogs for a walk. We'll have some breakfast when I get back which will give you sometime to wake up properly and get yourself dressed."

Rose disappeared off to her bedroom leaving Kate slowly sipping her tea.

Back in Goderich, Tom was also having his morning cup of tea while being propped up in bed. He still had small electrodes connected to a machine which showed a steady up and down graph that was monitoring his heart. All was good to the point that Tom wondered if there really was anything wrong with him at all?

At eight-thirty the nurse came in to get him ready for the ambulance saying, "We're going to give you a mild sedative, Mr. Blair so that you can sleep through the journey. The paramedics travelling with you will monitor everything so don't worry, you're in safe hands."

"Do I really have to be sedated?" Tom asked as he hated the idea of more drugs being pumped into his system.

"Well, I can give you just a very small dose enough to relax you, but not enough to knock you out completely. How does that sound?"

"Yes, that would be better, thanks." Tom said and then added as an after thought," Oh, and one more thing, could I bring my cell phone with me as I need to call my wife."

"I can't think that would be a problem, yes, sure. I'll give it to you. See, I've packed your belongings in a bag which will accompany you in the ambulance and I'll fish the phone out of it for you. Now, don't be using it until you're on the road, no phones are allowed in the wards."

Shortly afterwards Tom found himself being wheeled down the long hospital hallway on a gurney. Two strong looking paramedics lifted the stretcher into a waiting ambulance and then one of the men said impatiently, "Where on earth is Sean? I thought he was supposed to be on this shift?"

The other paramedic pulled out his walkie-talkie and held down the button as he spoke, "Call Sean McTavish, he's wanted on paramedic duty. Send him here asap."

The two men got into the front of the ambulance as soon as they saw the tardy paramedic appear in the lobby. He jumped into the back of the vehicle and closed the doors. The ambulance sped away on its way to London.

Tom lay back with his eyes closed feeling the drowsy soporific effects of the sedative. He was still connected to the heart monitor, but it was not uncomfortable. He felt himself slipping in and out of a drug-induced sleep. As his consciousness started to ebb, he opened his eyes and glanced at his fellow passenger. He could swear that he looked just like the man he had seen carrying the fishing rod case out at Windmill Lake. Maybe he was hallucinating. He closed his eyes and let the drugs take him.

THIRTY-THREE

I t was eight-fifty when Rose and Kate finally left Bayfield Terrace and headed for Highway 21. They had just reached Clan Gregor Square when Rose saw a red car driven by the very same woman with the mane of red hair who had banged into her car the previous night.

She was just about to pull away from the junction when Rose shouted, "That's her, that's the woman who drove into me last night and didn't have the decency to stop!"

"You should call the police," Kate said, "Look, I'll write down her license plate number and you can notify the OPP. Oh, but better still, Rose, we could pop into The Lion's Hall and speak to that hunky officer, DCI Hargreaves."

Rose smiled at her sister, "Well, if we're quick that probably would be the best option. I'll turn onto Cameron Street and double back to The Lion's Hall."

They were soon parked outside the hall and both women jumped out of the car and headed for the building. Rose knocked on the door and it was opened by a young female police officer who Rose recognized from the previous year.

Rose and Kate walked in and without further preamble blurted out,

"A woman in a red car," here Kate read out the license plate number," drove into my car last night when I was in Goderich. She was coming out of Britannia Road and failed to stop. Now we have just seen her pull out onto the highway from the Square."

"Okay, Rose, slow down a bit," John said, "You say that the car was red? Did you see the driver?"

She nodded and said, "Yes, the woman driving the car had a lot of red hair, and she appeared to be very small in build, probably in her forties."

The team exchanged a look of alarm.

"Did you say she was coming out of Britannia Street last night?"

"Yes, I was on my way to the hospital, oh, sorry John, you didn't know, but after you left us last night Tom felt really sick. I rushed him to the hospital and that's when the red car shot out of the blue and smashed into me."

"If I'm right, we know who the car belongs to and she's just taken off with a very valuable painting."

Rose couldn't understand what DCI Hargreaves was talking about as she knew nothing about a painting, but she didn't have time to question him.

"Look, I really have to get to London as Tom's having his surgery at twelve. All I wanted to do was to report that woman for not stopping after a car accident. I'll leave you to sort it out. By the way, she was heading south down the Highway towards Grand Bend. Right, I must go, bye everyone."

The team watched as Kate and Rose left the Lion's Hall. They were all still too stunned to talk.

THIRTY-FOUR

Anneka couldn't help but shout out in triumph, "I did it, I've got the painting!" Her plan had worked like clockwork and all those months of scheming had finally born fruit. Karel had played right into her hands. It was just a pity that he had to die. Now she would contact Gert who had rented a house in Grand Bend and had already settled right into the neighbourhood, even managing to set up his own studio.

Gert was eager to get his hands on the Vermeer again as his plan was to make several reproductions of *The Milkmaid* and flood the market so that no one person would ever know if they had the real deal or a forgery. He had brought with him, all the way from Holland, his collection of pigments and crushed stone. Indeed, his mortar and pestle had already been used to grind up several pieces of azurite and other rocks that he had purchased online. He had mixed the fine, ground rocks with various oils and ligaments to make a thick paint. He knew that his artwork would pass the most stringent of examinations as this had already been proven with Sotheby's on more than one occasion.

Anneka pulled into the Hessenland Inn car park and looked around her with interest. There was a vineyard to one side of the building and she could see more vines in the fields beyond.

Taking out her cell phone she texted Gert. He almost instantly replied giving her detailed instructions on how to get to his house. Anneka sighed, she would have to dump the car and soon; it felt as if she was driving a red beacon announcing where and who she was. Looking at the selection of cars parked next to her she wondered if anyone had left their keys in the ignition. Karel had told her that Canadians were too trusting as he had managed to steal two cars where both had ignition keys left inside.

She got out of her car and slowly walked past the parked cars, and trying not to make it too obvious, she looked through the window of each one. Very new cars had scrapped the use of keys altogether in favour of an electronic digital recognition system and so Anneka deliberately targeted older cars. The sixth car down the row of vehicles parked at The Hessenland carpark, had her shouting, "Bingo!" A large bunch of keys hung from the ignition. Anneka returned to her own car, grabbed her small travel case and the precious fishing rod canister, and hopped into the yellow VW Passat. In minutes she was back on the highway heading towards Grand Bend with a big smile on her face. *Gert, my babe, here I come*, she thought, *here I come.*

The ambulance made its way through Varna and then onto Brucefield. Tom slept and Karel dwelt upon making a plan for his future. Escaping from the hospital had been incredibly easy. He had feigned being comatose and had remained that way for most of the night knowing that he would be closely guarded. Karel assumed that he had been taken by ambulance to the hospital and it was this that gave him the idea for his escape. Fortunately, he had not been restrained, no hand cuffs, no monitor watching his every move; he was after all in a small rural hospital in an equally small town. He had truly lucked out big time on all fronts.

In the early hours of the morning, Karel had got out of bed, scrambled around for his clothes and then had crept out of the room. A policeman sat slumped over in a chair posted outside his room. He looked sound asleep and so Karel walked softly down the hospital corridor following the signs for the emergency. Just before entering the triage section, he noticed a couple of paramedics coming out of a room which had the word Staff on the door. Karel quietly pushed the door open and entered. There were a couple of paramedic jackets and fluorescent vests hanging from some pegs on the wall. He grabbed the closest to him and then shut himself in the washroom as much as anything to give himself time to think and plan his next action. If he could accompany a patient going out by ambulance then that would be his ticket out of the hospital.

It was by sheer luck then that he had overheard a couple of paramedics who had entered the staff room talking about the upcoming morning's schedule. An ambulance was due to leave the hospital to transport a man to St. Josephs Health Care in London at around eight-forty-five that morning. Karel would have to lay low for a while, but that was a small price to pay for his freedom. Two hours later, it had all gone to plan perfectly and now here he was sitting in the back of an ambulance trying to work out his next move.

Tom, meanwhile, had woken from his sleep and had once more glanced at the paramedic sitting opposite him. He certainly looked like the Dutchman he had seen at Windmill Lake, but what on earth would the man be doing dressed like a paramedic and, more to the point, accompanying him in the ambulance to London? None of it made any sense and so Tom reached under his blanket and found his phone which the very kind nurse had tucked in just before he left the ward. He would text Rose and elude to his suspicions about the paramedic, although she would probably think that he was hallucinating, but yet, stranger things had happened to him before in Bayfield.

Tom tapped in his message to Rose and pressed send. He had managed to work the phone discreetly, but he needn't really have worried as the paramedic was so intent on looking at his own cell phone that he did not notice what Tom was doing. He would have to wait to hear back from Rose, fortunately his phone was already set on vibrate and mute mode which hopefully would not draw any attention to Tom when Rose eventually returned his call. He closed his eyes and tried to go back to sleep although his mind could not stop trying to work out what Karel was doing in the ambulance with him.

THIRTY-FIVE

Rose and Kate had just reached Brucefield when Rose's phone blared out the opening tune of the 1812 Symphony, *da da da daaaa...da, da, da, daaaa.* Kate jumped in her seat and Rose laughed.

"It's just my phone, I chose that signature tune so that I couldn't ignore it. Look, I'm going to have to take the call, I'm sure that it will be Tom. I'm just going to pull over here."

They had reached the crossroads at Highway 4. Millington's Antiques was on the left-hand side and there was a small car park parked out front. Kate looked at the shop and said, "While you take your call, I think that I'll pop in here and have a quick look."

"Well, don't be too long, I don't want to be too far behind the ambulance."

Kate answered slightly impatiently. "Rose, even when Tom is admitted they will have to prep him for surgery which isn't until twelve and it's only nine thirty now. We've got plenty of time, don't worry."

"Okay, Kate, ten minutes and that's all."

Kate jumped out of the car and disappeared into the shop while Rose looked at the text message on her phone. Her mouth dropped when she saw Tom's message. How could Karel the Dutchman, be in the ambulance with Tom? It surely was not possible, but there was a niggling feeling in the pit of her stomach that made her reach for her phone and punch in DCI Hargreaves's number. Maybe he would be able to shed some light on it and, if nothing else, at least reassure her that it couldn't possibly be the Dutchman in the ambulance with Tom.

DCI Hargreaves answered the phone straight away.

"DCI Hargreaves speaking. How can I help you?"

"Oh, John, it's Rose Blair, look I've just had a rather disturbing message from Tom. He's on his way to London in an ambulance and he says that the Dutchman, you know the one wanted for murder? Well, he says that he is in the ambulance with him dressed up as a paramedic."

"That can't possibly be right. He was badly injured last night and admitted to the hospital. Look, let me check and see what the status on that is and I'll call you right back. Hold tight, I'll speak to you soon."

John put his phone down deep in thought and then he picked it up again and tapped in the hospital number. Immediately he could tell that there was some sort of panic and alert going on as he was put through to the hospital administrator who, after several attempts, finally told him that Karel de Vries had somehow escaped. They had looked everywhere for him in the hospital, but it was now clear that he had somehow just walked out all by himself. John was astounded at the lack of security and couldn't help himself blurt out, "But what about security cameras? Surely, for Pete's sake, you have those in the hospital?"

It was blatantly obvious that security was very lax, but for now John tried to keep his recriminations at bay. They had a killer on the loose in the community and it was then, and only then, that he remembered Rose Blair's conversation. *My God,* John thought, Karel was likely inside the ambulance with Tom Blair; he would have to handle this situation with the utmost care. He put the phone down and called his team together before he called Rose back.

THIRTY-SIX

Anneka found the address in Southcott Pines, Grand Bend and soon had parked the yellow VW Passat down the one side of the property; she would have to dump the car as soon as she could, but first she was more than anxious to see Gert.

Theirs had been a funny relationship right from the start. All four of them, Karel, Gerrit, Gert, and herself had attended the same high school in Gouda. Gerrit was older than the other three by two years and as a result had not got to know them well until several years later when both Gert and Karel left school to join Gerrit's father's business, Van Heuzen Art Restorers. Anneka had been the only one of the four who had pursued further education first by studying for a degree in Fine Art at Antwerp University followed by a Master's in the Old Dutch Masters and, finally, her doctorate in forensic art specialization. While she was finishing off her undergraduate studies Karel, Gerrit, and Gert had been dealing in forged paintings making meticulous reproductions executed by the very talented Gert. By the time Anneka had completed her master's all three men had been thrown into jail, Karel and Gerrit for twenty years and Gert for just ten years as he claimed to be just doing what he loved to do and that was to paint.

All through the men's imprisonment Anneka had visited them and on Gert's release she started a close relationship with him, although it was only in the past five years that they had fallen in love and began to plan for their future. The other two men, Karel and Gerrit were completely unaware of Gert and Anneka's relationship. In fact, it was decided that Anneka would cultivate an intimate relationship with Karel on his release. Gert had been privy to Gerrit and Karel's plans to retrieve the Vermeer painting which had been hidden inside the fishing rod case, indeed, he had actually crafted the forgery of *The Milkmaid*. The only draw back had been that the men had never told him where it was; they had hidden the painting and so it was imperative that Karel and Gerrit retrieve it and then Anneka would do the rest. He was now looking forward to getting reacquainted with the old painting again.

Anneka knocked on the front door of the rather dated 1980s split-level ranch house that Gert had rented. It was opened by Gert who had spent the past two hours nervously looking out of the lounge window anxiously waiting for Anneka's arrival.

"Come on in quickly. Oh, Anneka, I've been watching the local news channel and the police have let out all sorts of alert warnings for the public to lock their cars as there have been at least three car thefts in the past twenty-four hours."

He looked nervously outside to where Anneka had parked the yellow VW and said quickly, "That car needs to be put in the garage and now."

Anneka got back in the car and reversed while Gert

opened the garage doors. Once inside Anneka got out of the car and re-entered the house again through the internal garage door.

Gert rushed over, and, wrapping his arms around her he said, "Sorry, I've been so stressed waiting for you and when I heard about the stolen cars, I just about lost it. I've missed you so much," he whispered while he smelt the fragrance of her hair; she always used a lavender shampoo, and the light perfume on her skin, "but you won't be needing this anymore," and he pulled off her shaggy mane of red hair, a wig they had agreed that she would wear, underneath which she sported a short pixie hair cut which suited her elfin features far more than the mass of red hair.

"Did Karel not even suspect that you were wearing a wig?"

Anneka shook her head saying, "Well, I've been wearing this for quite a while now, back in Amsterdam I've got a shorter version, but to be honest I'm more than happy to get rid of it particularly in this heat."

"Right, now I want to devour every inch of your amazing body and then I want to get reacquainted with Vermeer."

Gert lifted Anneka up in his arms and carried her through to the bedroom. He closed the door quietly.

THIRTY-SEVEN

They were nearing London and had just driven through Arva when Karel hit upon a plan that he felt confident would work. He had an Uber app on his cell phone. He scrolled through the list of drivers available and found one based right next to the hospital. He texted the driver and waited for an answer which came through within minutes. Yes, the driver would meet him in the hospital car park right by the Emergency entrance where the ambulances parked. The Uber driver was prepared to drive Karel to Grand Bend. The bitch, Anneka, Karel thought, had foolishly left her cell phone on, and he had been able to use the phone's GPS to track her down at an address in a place called Southcott Pines in Grand Bend. All he needed now was some sort of weapon. He looked around the inside of the ambulance to see if he could find anything that he could improvise as a weapon. There was a bright red zippered bag sitting on the floor and when Karel unzipped it, he found a whole load of medical supplies from syringes to bandages, vials of opiates, and a defibrillator. All perfect, he thought, perfect for what he had in mind.

The ambulance pulled into the Emergency rear entrance of St. Joseph's Hospital. Karel prepared to jump out the minute the vehicle stopped.

Rose and Kate had made record time and got to the hospital five minutes before the ambulance. They had parked their car as close as possible to the ambulance entrance and sat and waited.

Rose said seriously, "We really should let them admit Tom first before we go in ourselves." Just as Rose was speaking, the back door to the ambulance burst open and Karel jumped out carrying a red bag.

"Good God Rose, that's Karel! Tom was right, he is dressed like a paramedic. What on earth is he doing now?"

A car pulled up alongside Karel and he jumped in and the car started to leave the hospital car park.

"Quick, Rose, quick. Follow that car." Kate yelled.

Rose put the car into reverse and then proceeded to follow the car in front shouting to her sister to take down the license plate number and then to phone DCI Hargreaves. She had never tailed a vehicle before but, having watched a load of cop shows, knew that she had to somehow keep her distance and not make it too obvious that she was following them.

Thoughts of Tom flashed through her mind. She should be with him now and not going on some wild goose chase.

They were pretty well retracing the same route taken driving into London, back onto Richmond to Mason Ville, across the lights at Fanshaw Park Road, and up on through Arva, Lucan, and on to Exeter. Kate had finally got hold of DCI Hargreaves and full alert had been dispatched to all OPP officers.

John told Kate to be extremely careful and not to do anything rash, "Just keep your distance and as soon as we have you in our sights, we will take over the tailing."

They reached the set of traffic lights at the corner of Highway 83 and 8, the car being tailed turned left.

"I reckon they're heading to Grand Bend," Kate said, "That strange woman with all that hair looked as if she was heading for Grand Bend too."

Rose looked at her watch, Tom's surgery was scheduled for twelve and it was already ten past eleven. If she was to turn around and head back to London now, she could possibly make it in time.

"Kate, could you contact DCI Hargreaves again please and ask where they are?"

After a brief conversation with the detective, it was ascertained that Sergeant Flowers and Constable Elliot were on Airport Line very close to Highway 83. They had also dispatched a car directly to Grand Bend and it would be parked in the car park by the traffic lights ready to take up the tailing of the car from there should it appear in Grand Bend. Constable Ryan and been on the internet to the DRV and discovered that the owner of the license plate was an Uber driver and regularly taxied people around London. Karel must have booked him from the ambulance.

Rose was approaching Airport Road; she pulled over and grabbed the phone from Kate, "John, I must get back to London to the hospital. I'm at the crossroads between Airport Road and Highway 83. Your Sergeant cannot be far. Tell him to turn right at the junction and head for Grand Bend. If he's lucky he'll probably be able to catch the driver as he's not going super fast."

John knew that Rose was worried about Tom and his

impending surgery and there was certainly no point in endangering the public anymore particularly as they had it all in hand.

He thanked her and was about to end the call when Rose said, "Oh and John, please be careful. Could you let me know the outcome when this is all over? I feel somehow responsible for part of this craziness, certainly by encouraging my sister to go on a date with him." John smiled and said that he would let her know what transpired, but not to get her hopes too high.

With that out of the way Rose pulled the car back onto the road and indicated that she was turning left onto Airport Line on route for London and to her beloved husband, Tom.

THIRTY-EIGHT

Karel opened the red bag that he had taken from the ambulance and inside he pulled out the little vials of morphine and fentanyl, a small oxygen canister and mask, plus a defibrillator, a blanket, and rolls of bandages, not an awful lot that he could use as a murder weapon. He did, however, have one huge ace up his sleeve and that was the complete element of surprise. Anneka thought that he was dead and not in a million years would she be expecting to see him again.

He looked at the time, it was eleven forty-five, almost midday, he would be, according to his GPS in Grand Bend by twelve. Once again, he surveyed the contents of the medical bag. If he could inject large enough doses of either of the contents of the vials, than that would surely be deadly enough. The oxygen tank could be used to bludgeon someone to death, but that would be messy and take some effort. No, he needed something much cleaner and quicker like a garrote. Maybe the bandages could be twisted together to form a rope of sorts; now that would be much easier to manage. He would fill the syringes as well, just in case strangulation didn't quite work. Using the remaining fifteen minutes of his journey he twisted several rolls of bandages together and then filled several syringes with morphine and fentanyl. He glanced at the driver who had not uttered a single word to him since picking him up outside the hospital. He would get the man to drop him off just around the corner from his destination in Southcott Pines, just in case he was being tracked by the police plus he did not want to raise the alarm by pulling up in Anneka's driveway.

The car slowed down as it approached an intersection with Highway 21. There was a sign pointing to The Huron Playhouse and another billboard advertising a drive-in movie theatre. They drove past a shop called Sea Jewells and then a larger establishment called Home Hardware. Soon they were in a semi built up area having passed a golf-course called The Oakwood, a Tim Horton's, and The Colonial Hotel. At the traffic lights Karel could see what presumably was the Main Street of Grand Bend which was heaving with tourists some very scantily attired in bikinis and other swim wear. This was obviously a holiday vacation town and by the looks of things, one busy destination. Another time Karel might have enjoyed a visit, but today he was on a mission, one that had to be completed and soon.

Unbeknown to him, a black Chevrolet Impala pulled out behind the Uber driver and proceeded to follow them. The driver indicated that he was turning right off the highway into Southcott Pines. Karel prepared himself, the time had come, vengeance would be sweet.

Anneka and Gert were still in bed. After her arrival and the initial excitement and euphoria of viewing the Vermeer together, they had made passionate love and then had both fallen into a deep, satiated sleep. It was Gert who woke up first, stretching his arms above his head, he turned his head sideways to look at Anneka who was still sound asleep. She looked so young and vulnerable particularly with her short haircut.

He had initially been very shocked to hear that she had cold heartedly killed Karel as that had not been part of their plan, but there again, the murder of Gerrit had not been their idea either. Now all that really mattered was the painting. He needed to reproduce several copies of *The Milkmaid*, and then both Anneka and he had to sell off the original to the highest bidder before they flooded the market with the forgeries. They had found a potential buyer, an American from Las Vegas, who had put in a bid for thirty-five million dollars. They had hoped to get at least forty million, but maybe they would just cut their losses, accept the offer, and then disappear. *But where to*, Gert thought. He had spent all of his life living in Holland, admittedly ten miserable years had been spent in prison, but he was essentially still just a homebody, didn't like change and just longed to settle down with the woman of his dreams, Anneka.

Of course, she could never go back to the Rijks Museum, indeed she would never, ever be able to work as an art specialist again, well, at least not in Europe. That was a real waste to the world as her knowledge of the Old Dutch Masters was second to none on the global front. But, if they succeeded in selling the Vermeer, they could choose to settle anywhere in the world, the furthest away possible, maybe New Zealand or somewhere in the South Pacific. Memories of paintings by Gauguin flickered through Gert's mind and he found himself

picturing a white, sandy beach with coconut palms and beautiful Tahitian women dancing around him.

Feeling suddenly much better having visualized living on
an exotic island, he quietly got himself dressed in his running
gear, shorts, t-shirt, and running shoes. He would go for a quick
run as was his usual routine, swing by Tim Horton's and pick
up two coffees to-go, and then come back and cook a late
breakfast, or brunch, as the Americans were apt to say.

Gert let himself out of the back door and quickly ran
across the grass towards the beach totally oblivious to the man
stealthily approaching the front of his house.

Karel tried opening the front door; it was locked just as he
had expected, but twenty years in prison had taught him a few
tricks. He always carried a set of master keys on him wherever
he went never knowing when he might need to use them.
Easing one key in the lock after another, suddenly he felt a
click and knew that he was in. Quietly, he entered the silent
house and found himself in a lobby which was open plan to a
large living room, kitchen, and dining room where two doors
faced him at the end of a short corridor.

Karel slowly walked towards one of the doors; he opened it
very softly and found himself in a spacious bedroom. The light
in the room was dimmed by closed blinds, he could just make
out a king-sized bed with someone lying asleep on it. Karel
approached the bed realizing that it was indeed Anneka and
he could not help but observe just how beautiful she looked in
repose, although he was initially shocked to see her with short,
spikey hair. His resolve was softened briefly until his eyes lit
upon the fishing rod case. He picked the case up and tiptoed
out of the bedroom. He would check that the Vermeer was still
there before he dealt with Anneka.

Finding the painting rolled up and tucked inside the case,

he left it in the living room intending to pick it up on his way out. He returned to the bedroom just as Anneka's eyes fluttered open. Karel lurched forward, his make-shift rope in hand, the syringes in his pocket, and grabbed Anneka by the neck.

THIRTY-NINE

Sergeant Flowers and Constable Elliot had watched Karel enter the house in Southcott Pines. They were quietly parked behind a tree on the road in front of the house just waiting for their boss, DCI Hargreaves, to give the word for them to proceed. Constable Elliot fidgeted with his weapon feeling more than anxious as he had never had to use a gun, but at the same time knowing that Karel de Vries had already murdered one person and attempted to murder another, it still made him feel distinctly uncomfortable. A flash of movement through the trees on the road back the way they had come indicated that DCI Hargreaves was on his way. They would soon be able to proceed although there was still no sign of Karel leaving the house and they had no idea what he was up to inside.

The two officers got out of their car as DCI Hargreaves and Constable Ryan pulled up beside them. They walked over and waited for their boss to reveal his plan of action.

John got out and looked at the house saying, "Sergeant, you

reported that our man has just gone inside the building about five minutes ago, is that correct?"

"Yes, sir, but he hasn't come out yet. Do we know who lives here?"

"Constable Ryan has just checked online and a Gert Dupuis is currently renting the property through Bluewater Rentals."

Sergeant Flowers listened to the information and appeared deep in thought. "The name Gert Dupuis rings a bell, sir. Wasn't he part of the trio that made up the Van Heuzen scam? If I remember correctly, he was the master painter."

Constable Ryan had opened up her laptop and was revisiting her notes on the Van Heuzen case. Suddenly she let out a gasp saying, "You're right, Gert Dupuis was the master artist and he, too, was imprisoned, but whereas Karel and Gerrit got twenty years, Gert only received ten years. He was released twelve years ago on parole and for the past ten years he's been completely off the radar. It doesn't say here how long he's been in Canada, but that won't be hard to find out."

DCI Hargreaves nodded his head sagely saying, "So, we have Karel stealthily breaking into Gert's house, his old partner in crime. What's he up to and why all the stealth? The only way we'll find out is by going in ourselves. Right are you all ready? Have your weapons at hand."

FORTY

Gert felt all hot and sweaty after his run and was about to sprint up to the front door when he checked himself just in time. There, in the front of his house, were two parked cars, unmarked police cars by the looks of things. There was a huddle of four people conferring by the vehicles. He paused and decided to run around to the back of the house and slip in through the back door. He quietly let himself in and was about to go upstairs when he suddenly heard footsteps. Maybe Anneka was awake, but the footsteps sounded much heavier than they should for a woman only one hundred pounds in weight.

Gert softly padded into the living room, the fishing rod case lay on the floor, he was sure that it had been in the bedroom before, but he did not waste any more time thinking about it. Grabbing the case he pulled the canvas out and left the empty cylinder on the floor. Very quietly he left the building. He would text Anneka as soon as he could, just as soon as the cars had gone. Some gut instinct had told him to lay low himself as Anneka was more than capable of looking after herself and so he quietly ran through the back garden and back down towards the beach. He would give it an hour before returning to the house.

Karel grabbed Anneka's short, spikey hair and yanked her up into a sitting position. Once again, he couldn't resist eyeing her body in a completely lascivious way, lustfully taking in the delicious shape of her breasts, the glow of her skin, the curve of her hips, and her long, sexy legs. It all seemed such a waste of a fine body, but the bitch truly deserved to die and die she would very soon, Karel thought.

Anneka fought like a wild tiger, biting Karel's fingers and kicking him so hard that he had to resort to sitting on top of her writhing body and clamping his hand down hard on her mouth expelling all air from her lungs. Tying the makeshift rope around her neck he whispered his final farewell and started to pull the rope tightly. Anneka's eyes began to bulge and her feet pounded the bed while the rest of her body lay immobilized by the weight of Karel straddled across her. Her eyes started to roll back into her head and her face turned a violent crimson.

She was just a few seconds away from death when DCI Hargreaves and Sergeant Flowers burst into the room shouting, "Police. Stand away and put your hands in the air, weapons on the ground. Do it now!"

Sergeant Flowers stood firmly; his gun trained on Karel ready to shoot at any provocation. Karel slowly got off Anneka and stood up eyeing the two men in front of him. He heard the sound of feet running and seconds later two more officers appeared, one of them a young woman who looked at him nervously.

"Are you alright, guv?" she said and the older of the two men replied quickly,

"Yes, Constable, all good, but I'm not sure about this

woman here." John used his head to indicate the body of a naked woman lying motionless in the middle of the bed. Holly ran over to Anneka and felt for a pulse at the same time she covered her body with the sheet.

"I think that she's breathing, guv, but it's very shallow. I'll call for an ambulance."

"Thank you, Constable. Now, handcuff this man and take him to the car. Sergeant, search the house."

Anneka's eyes had fluttered open and her body shuddered violently with delayed shock. She tried to talk but nothing came out. Her hand raised to her throat and she pulled away the remnants of the bandage that had been used to strangle her. Constable Ryan called to DCI Hargreaves. "Guv, this woman here is none other than Dr. Moleevaar. It's just the short hair that threw us."

"Good God, you're quite right, it is Dr. Moleevaar. What on earth is she doing here with Karel and where is Gert Dupuis?"

"Guv, there is a connection, you know. Dr. Moleevaar worked at the Rijks Museum and Karel, Gerrit, and Gert all worked on restoring and ultimately, forging the Old Dutch Masters. They could all have met then, maybe?"

The sound of the ambulance siren pierced the air and soon two paramedics appeared and within minutes they had Anneka strapped to a stretcher and taken out to the waiting vehicle.

DCI Hargreaves spoke quickly, "Constable Ryan I would like you to accompany the patient, but don't let her out of your sight whatever you do. Just as soon as she's been checked over, I want her at the head office in London, is that clear?"

"Yes, guv," Constable Ryan said and hopped into the back of the ambulance.

Sergeant Flowers returned to the room carrying the fishing rod case.

"I found it in the living room, sir, but I'm afraid that it's empty."

DCI Hargreaves threw his arms in the air feeling thoroughly exasperated.

"That weasel Gert must have taken the painting. Look, we'll find him, but right now I'm leaving you in charge here, Sergeant while I escort our murderer to London with Constable Elliot. I won't be back until tomorrow; I'll write this all up then. Could you put out all the necessary procedures for a search for Gert Dupuis? Has the car been found, the stolen VW Passat?"

"Yes, sir, it's in the garage."

"Well, at least we've managed to retrieve all the stolen vehicles and they are all still intact, which is one good thing. Okay, I'm on my way; I'll see you tomorrow."

DCI Hargreaves walked to where Constable Elliot waited beside the car. Karel de Vries was handcuffed and sitting subdued inside the vehicle.

"Okay, Constable, you get to drive, I want to question this scumbag."

FORTY-ONE

Rose and Kate got to St. Joseph's Health Care Centre just in time to see Tom being wheeled into surgery. Rose was able to squeeze his hand and kiss him gently as the trolley rolled past them and then the endless waiting began. Kate fetched them both coffee from the Tim Horton's booth set up inside the hospital and Rose paced the floor of the waiting room anxiously scanning the theatre for any signs of either a doctor or a nurse or indeed anyone at all who could give her any information about Tom. One hour into her wait there appeared to be tremendous activity going on inside and outside the operating room and four doctors and nurses came running to the theatre.

"What's going on, please someone tell me what's happening?" Rose appealed to one of the nurses who was about to dive into the theatre.

"It looks like someone's gone into cardiac arrest,"

Rose went quite pale, "Oh, my God, it's Tom, my Tom."

Kate rushed to her sister and hugged her tight guiding her to a chair where she made Rose sit.

"Rose, now listen, Tom is in excellent hands, he'll be alright, but maybe you should call the girls and Paul."

She nodded feebly and with shaking hands as she pulled out her phone and then she noticed a large sign on the wall forbidding the use of cell phones in the hospital.

"Kate, could you go outside and call the kids for me. I can't use my phone inside and I just don't want to leave the waiting room area in case..." here Rose's voice began to break and Kate squeezed her shoulders and told her that she would deal with the family.

"Hold on in there, darling. Tom will be fine; I just know it."

Thirty minutes later Paul rushed into the waiting room and hugged his mother tightly. His voice thickened as he said, "How is Dad? Aunt Kate said that he'd gone into cardiac arrest. Mom, is Mad going to be okay?"

Rose was about to answer Paul when the door to the operating theatre suddenly burst open and a doctor wearing theatre scrubs walked over to where Rose and Paul were sitting.

"Mrs. Blair, can I have a word with you?"

Rose nodded bravely fearing the worst.

"Your husband had a small set back in there but he's doing just fine now. We're just moving him back to the ward where you can see him."

Rose let out a deep breath. "Thank God, thank God, and thank you."

Kate put her arms around her sister and hugged her and then the theatre door swung open again and the gurney holding Tom was wheeled out. He was attached to a number of tubes connected to an IV unit which was pulled along on a separate carrier by a nurse. His eyes were closed, but his skin colouring was good. Rose let out a deep sigh of relief and began to follow the gurney into the ward. Paul and Kate followed a few steps behind. They had just reached the recovery ward when Rose's phone started to ring. She checked to see who the call was from and saw that it was DCI Hargreaves. She turned her phone off and continued to follow the gurney. Tom was in recovery and that was all that mattered. The whole mystery and intrigue surrounding the murder at Windmill Lake had paled into insignificance to Rose compared to the life of her beloved husband, Tom. DCI Hargreaves would have to wait as Tom was all that mattered.

FORTY-TWO

On the road to London, DCI Hargreaves started the interview process. He took out his phone and set it to record mode placing it on the seat between Karel and himself.

"This is DCI Hargreaves interviewing Karel de Vries on this day Thursday, July 19, 2019. Right, tell me about Dr. Moleevaar."

Karel turned and spat at the detective.

"Oh, so you want to play it like that, do you my sonny?"

Before Karel could reply John swiftly pushed his head down onto his knees and grabbed his cuffed hands twisting them together like a knot. Karel let out a yelp and John continued to tighten the knot harder whispering in his ear as he did so, "You play ball with me, sonny, or it will be your balls next." He yanked Karel back up into sitting position and smiled at him saying, "Right, let's start again, shall we? Tell me all you know about Dr. Moleevaar?"

Karel coughed, stuttered, and chewed his lip before he

replied, but when he finally started to talk, it was like a flood of water coming out of a burst faucet.

"Anneka, Gerrit, Gert, and I all attended the same high school, we hung out together and were best of friends. Gerrit's dad owned his own business, Van Heuzen Art Restoration, so when we left school Gert and I joined Gerrit working for his dad. Gert was a brilliant painter, but as to Anneka, well she went off to university, studied art, and finally got her doctorate.

"By the time we were working the trade and the year we were caught, Anneka had secured a really good position at The Rijks Museum in Amsterdam. She never had anything to do with the heist, in fact, we never told her any specifics about the forgeries. It was when all three of us were imprisoned that we got close, just Anneka and me. She visited me once a week and we talked about art and I hinted that Gerrit and I might know something about the whereabouts of a certain Vermeer, but I couldn't openly say anything while locked up. She stuck by me all those years and when I was released, we really got together, if you know what I mean, and I told her everything, I mean everything. She urged me to return to Canada and retrieve the painting, but I told her that Gerrit wouldn't let me claim it for myself. It was her idea to kill Gerrit and then the sodding bitch tried to murder me, go figure."

"What about Gert Dupuis? Where does he feature in all of this?"

Karel looked blank, "Gert doesn't feature in any of this. I lost contact with him years ago. He got out of prison after ten years and never once visited either Gerrit or me. He just disappeared, never got in touch with us, just faded off the face of the earth. So, why do you ask, what has he got to do with any of this?"

He obviously didn't know about Anneka and Gert, John

thought and that was interesting. It was apparent that Gert had taken the Vermeer and both Karel and Anneka were oblivious to the fact. He continued to ask Karel more questions.

"So, tell me about the painting you hid in the fishing rod case? Where exactly is it now?"

Karel snarled like a rabid dog as he shouted, "That bitch Anneka double crossed me. She stole the fishing-rod case after trying to suffocate me. That painting is worth millions."

"Okay, calm down now. How were you going to sell the painting?"

"Anneka had it all worked out. She had already contacted several existing clients of the Rijks Museum who had expressed interest in the Old Dutch Masters. You would be surprised at the number of collectors that there are out there; some living in obscure countries, but wealthy as creases. She never confided in me as to who was going to purchase the painting only that we would be getting forty million. As far as I was concerned that was incentive enough."

"Right, one more question before we're finished here, where did you procure the gun?"

Karel sneered again as he replied and John wanted to slap the man in the face but managed to restrain himself in time.

"You mean to say you pigs can't work that out for yourself? Well, I'll tell you. Twenty-two years ago security wasn't that great at airports and I managed to hide the gun inside my fishing rod case along with the rolled-up canvas. Gerrit knew nothing about it. The gun was an old Luger 5, my father's war time gun which I preloaded with bullets and also slipped into the case a small plastic pop bottle over the muzzle to act as a silencer. I stashed the whole lot away and when I retrieved the fishing rod case years later it was easy. I slipped my hand in, pulled out the gun, turned and shot Gerrit all in one quick motion. I must admit to being pleasantly surprised that it all worked after this many years."

John had to once again restrain himself. *The smarmy, smug bastard was actually proud of himself and showed no remorse for his actions at all,* he thought as he turned off his phone and sat looking straight ahead feeling how dirty it felt sitting next to the scumbag, Karel.

They reached the outskirts of London and would soon be arriving at the Serious Crimes Unit Head Quarters on Richmond Street. John would try phoning Rose Blair one more time.

FORTY-THREE

Rose, Paul, and Kate sat around the bed where Tom lay peacefully asleep. The doctor had conducted his rounds and had declared everything, all his vitals, to be good. He suggested that the family go home to rest as Tom would probably sleep another twelve hours at least.

Paul invited his mother and aunt to go back to his small apartment to stay, but Rose declined saying,

"The dogs, dear, need to be looked after and I'm hopeless sleeping in someone else's bed. But thank you darling for your kind offer. You need to go home to Atsuko and baby Yuki. Kate and I will drive back to Bayfield and I'll return tomorrow morning."

They had just reached the car park when Rose's phone rang. It was DCI Hargreaves.

"Hi Rose, I wanted to let you know that thanks to you we have successfully apprehended our suspects. Both Karel de Vries and Dr. Moleevaar are in custody. How are you doing? How is Tom?"

Rose was touched that DCI Hargreaves had taken the time

to call her and that he had enquired after Tom.

"He's doing alright, John. Kate's with me and we're about to head back home."

"Would you like to meet me for an early dinner or is it a late lunch, maybe in twenty minutes or so?"

Rose looked at her watch and then at Kate. They had both skipped breakfast and lunch and were starving. If they made it a quick meal, they would still be home in time to feed the dogs.

"Yes, we would love to. Where should we meet?"

"Well, I know there's a lovely Italian restaurant in Byron but whether it's open so early, I'm not so sure. There's a Kelsey's on Commissioners or there's an authentic Greek restaurant on Albert Street right downtown. What do you fancy?"

"The Greek restaurant sounds great. Okay, we'll head there now and see you soon. What was the name?"

"I think that it's called The Mythic Grill. It's fabulous, really authentic, you'll enjoy it I'm sure."

Kate and Rose hugged Paul goodbye and got into the car. It took them only ten minutes to get to Albert Street and so they parked the car and decided to spend twenty minutes looking at the shops on Richmond Street. There was a book shop that Rose had visited before and so they made a beeline for it although Kate would have preferred to have been clothes shopping. They whiled away twenty minutes in a flash and were soon back at The Mystic Grill seated and waiting for John to arrive. The ambiance was great, Greek music played in the background, crusty bread and dipping oils sat on the tables, and most handsome waiters hovered in the background. Kate and Rose were eager to grab the bread and get started and were just about to when John walked into the room.

Kate whispered to Rose, "My, he's a handsome man, isn't

he?" Rose smiled and stood up beckoning to John to join them at their table. He strode over to them and gave both women big hugs.

"So, have you ordered yet?"

The next ten minutes were spent chatting away amicably while they waited for their drinks order to arrive.

Rose asked John about the case saying, "Are you at liberty to discuss it with us now that you've wrapped up the case?"

John laughed, "Well, I suppose I can tell you the bare bones as long as you don't spread it to the whole of Bayfield."

He proceeded to tell Kate and Rose the details ending with the fact that the fishing rod case found in the house was empty.

"So, I was right all along, there was a canvas painting inside. Did you find out what the canvas was, John?"

Kate nudged her sister and said, "Hey, I'm the one that found the canvas inside the fishing rod case, I just didn't know what it was."

"You were both right and my sincere gratitude to you both. We do know that the painting was a famous Vermeer called *The Milkmaid*, and our art specialist, Dr. Moleevaar was in partnership with Gert Dupuis who was also the master painter of reproductions. They planned to sell the Vermeer to a collector. Gert must have somehow sneaked into the house when we were arresting Karel and stole the painting. Anyway, as soon as I've finished up here, I have a meeting with the chief, a debriefing, and then I'm going home to get some well-earned kip. I'll be back in the village tomorrow to debrief the team and so I won't say goodbye just yet, besides I would like to visit Tom when he gets back home. Give him my regards for now."

Kate and Rose left soon after they had finished their meal; they had an hour's journey ahead and two hungry dogs waiting for them back home.

FORTY-FOUR

Gert ran to the lock up storage unit he had rented a few weeks ago. He had wanted somewhere to store all his art equipment while he set up his studio. He had also purchased a motor bike on Kijiji, a Honda 750 which was ten years old, but in excellent condition. Back in Amsterdam he had both a pedal bicycle and a motor bike; like most people in the city he used the pedal bike, but for travelling out of the city he loved nothing better than to let loose on his motor bike and hit the highways. What he loved about Canada was the vastness and the emptiness of the roadways, once one escaped the cities.

Gert looked around at his storage unit and soon spied what he was looking for, his artists carrying tube which was far less bulky than the fishing-rod case and could easily be tied to the back of the Honda. He found his backpack too but decided against bringing it as he had nothing to put in it. When he reached his destination there would be time enough to purchase all the necessities, but right now he was just interested in putting in the distance away from Grand Bend as quickly as possible.

Vancouver would take at least four days to reach. Fortunately, he had the presence of mind to have hidden his false passport in a mini safe inside the lock up. Both Anneka and he had planned to change their identities for the last part of their plan. He would leave Anneka's passport in the lock up and text her the security number for the keyboard. Momentarily he wondered what was happening back in the house. Anneka had always told him not to look back in any situation and he was doing just that as he had every faith in Anneka's resourcefulness, but he was also a realist. If anything had happened to her it would be up to him to continue with their plan and that he would do come what may.

Checking his wallet and replacing his existing I.D. under the name of Gert Dupuis with that of Piet de Groot, his passport, driving license, credit cards, and health insurance all now bore his new name. Piet took one more look around his lock-up and then, tying the artist's canister holding the precious Vermeer onto the back of his bike, he started the engine and motored off in the direction of Park Hill and the motorway.

BACK IN BAYFIELD, Rose was welcomed home by two hungry and extremely anxious dogs and a barrage of phone messages left on the answer machine. First a very frantic Jessica left a message demanding that Rose call her right away with the status of her father. A second message was also anxiously enquiring after her father, but less strident than her sister, Anne concluded with she was thinking about Rose and to please tell Dad that she loved him very much. There were half a dozen messages from well-meaning friends of Rose and Tom including one from Doug, Tom's golfing partner. She would contact them all later but right now the dogs needed to be fed and walked and Rose desperately wanted to creep into bed and sleep. She felt absolutely drained of energy and was physically and mentally exhausted.

KATE HAD ALSO WALKED into her small house feeling thoroughly exhausted too. It had been a frantic day full of emotional ups and downs and all she wanted to do right now was to run a hot bath and soak in it before crashing out in bed. Tomorrow she would go to the animal rescue and bring little Lucy home with her. If the past few days had taught her anything it was to live life to its fullest and with no regrets because you never knew what was around the corner. Even Karel had asked her why she was hesitating when it was so obvious that she was totally besotted by Lucy.

"I love Lucy," Kate shouted out loud, "I love lucy!"

Thinking of Karel gave Kate pause for thought. Although she never, ever wanted to relive that dreadful date, it had taught her something important and that was she was ready to start dating. Now that her body had been sexually aroused, she craved the intimacy of skin upon skin and human touch. Somehow John Hargreaves's handsome face flashed through her mind. Had she sensed any chemistry between them at all? She would have to wait and see and if not, she would follow her sister's advice and start online dating and maybe even try some speed dating. With that thought in mind Kate climbed into bed and closed her eyes and, within minutes, she was out like a light.

FORTY-FIVE

DCI Hargreaves went straight back to the Serious Crimes Head Office after saying his farewells to Rose and Kate. They had had a great time together and he had felt totally relaxed and at ease with their company. Both women intrigued him, but in totally different ways. Kate was still so vulnerable and bruised from her marriage break up. He sensed that given time she would emerge like a beautiful butterfly from a chrysalis, but for now he felt he wouldn't be able to handle his own grief as well as someone else's.

Rose, on the other hand, was a different matter. She was forbidden fruit in many ways being married and, seemingly happily to Tom, yet of the two women, it was Rose's face that he pictured in his dreams. Shaking those thoughts away, John concentrated on the interview ahead. Karel was no problem in terms of booking him, he had all but confessed to the murder of Gerrit Van Heuzen. However, John was more worried about Anneka Moleevaar. So far, she had refused to talk to anyone. He had gone over his notes and there was little in terms of concrete evidence to show that she had attempted to murder

Karel de Vries. Any lawyer worth their salt would be able to cut through Anneka's story like butter. Indeed, the only concrete evidence of misbehavior or crime was the stolen car and the hit and run with Rose Blair's Volvo. He was waiting, now, to meet with his boss, the Commissionaire, to sort out what to do about Dr. Moleevaar.

FORTY-SIX

Gert Dupuis, now Piet de Groot, on the 401 just outside Mississauga, stopped at the service station. He went into the food court and took his place in a line up at the Tim Horton's concession. In his short time living in Canada he had quickly come to realize that the coffee shop was very much part of Canadian culture. He had heard that Timmy's was opening shops in Europe which would give Costa Coffee a run for their money.

Whilst queuing he pulled out his cell phone and texted Anneka again, this time using the name Piet de Groot. She would instantly know who he was as it had been her original plan to obtain the false passwords and I.D. under different names. For the hundredth time Gert wondered what had happened to Anneka, he just hoped that she was physically alright, he knew that mentally she would survive just fine with her sharp wit and smart brain.

He had marked out a route that he would take and that was basically to follow the Trans Canadian Highway all the way to Vancouver. He planned to keep driving until at least ten o'clock that night hoping to possibly make Thunder Bay before checking into a motel. At least it was summertime and it would not get dark much before nine thirty or so and the mornings were light too so he could get an early start.

Yes, he should get to Vancouver, all barring any unforeseen delays, in three days time, four at the very most. It would be good to see the ocean again. Sitting at a table with his steaming hot cup of Tim Horton's, a chicken sandwich, and a Boston Crème donut in front of him, Gert thought once again about Anneka.

Did she really love him or was she just using him because of his painting skills, not to mention the priceless Vermeer? It seemed incredible to think that it had only been four hours since they had made love so passionately and had laid spent on his bed in the house in Southcott Pines.

It was a shame as he had liked living there and would miss the wooded neighbourhood and the lovely beach where he regularly ran each morning. The studio he had so painstakingly set up would now never be used and all the pigments and paints he had prepared would all go to waste. Maybe he had overreacted, but his gut instinct had told him to run, plus Anneka had always told him to never take chances and to go to Plan B at the slightest hint of something not right. He checked his phone again, still no reply from Anneka. Finishing his sandwich and coffee he wrapped the donut up in a napkin and stuffed it in his pocket and then went outside leaving the lovely cool air-conditioned building for the heat of the July afternoon. He climbed onto his motor bike and kicked-started the machine. The engine roared fiercely as Gert drove away back onto the 401.

D CI Hargreaves slammed his fists down hard onto the desk in his office at the Serious Crimes Head Quarters in London. He had just left the Commissionaires office after a long discussion about Dr. Moleevaar. It had been decided that she would be released from custody as the Commissionaire did not want any political fallout with a Dutch national on Canadian ground. He defended his case by saying that she had said in a written statement that the attempted murder was nothing more than kinky sex gone wrong, and that Karel had agreed to being tied up. The plastic bag suffocation was supposed to heighten sexual awareness. In other words, Dr. Moleevaar had an answer for everything, and DCI Hargreaves felt that his hands were tied.

As to Karel de Vries, it had been decided that he would be deported back to Holland where he would stand trial for the murder of Gerrit Van Heuzen, although the weasel, after confessing all in the car driving to London, had now retracted everything he had said saying that he had been undue duress at the time. Obviously he had conferred with a lawyer who must have advised him that without an actual gun or any fingerprints or, indeed, any conclusive evidence that tied him to the murder other than the two men being friends, the case would have to go to court in Holland where it would be analysed and probably reinvestigated. DCI Hargreaves had left the building feeling suitably battered and in doubt of the whole legal system. He drove back to his house and immediately telephoned his daughter, Rachael.

"Oh, hi Dad, what's up?"

"Nothing, darling, just wanted to hear your lovely voice. I've just finished up a case and I'm feeling a tad low in spirits, that's all."

"But Dad, you should be out celebrating if you've tied up a case. What's the problem?"

Rachael knew him so well. She could tell from his tone of voice that he was frustrated. He told her all about the case and how Dr. Moleevaar had got off being convicted and how the Dutchman was trying to wheedle out of his conviction.

"Where's the justice system gone, Rachael, honestly it makes me so angry."

"Oh Dad, calm down, it sounds as if you did your job. It's not your fault that the two of them haven't received due justice. Look, do you want to pop over for a drink?"

John looked at his watch and was shocked to see that it was so late, already ten thirty. He thanked his daughter, but declined her offer, instead, after he had put the phone down, he poured himself out a large scotch and took it into the living room. He turned on the television, he was far too wired up to go to bed just yet, a bit of television would calm him down.

FORTY-EIGHT

A nneka was discharged that same evening and, as she stood on the sidewalk in front of the Serious Crimes building, she pondered her options. First and foremost, she had to check her phone as Gert must have been worried sick about her. His first text message announced that he would be back in one hour and then there were a number of messages from a Piet de Groot whom she instantly recognized as the pseudonym for Gert. According to his texts he was on the road riding his motor bike and would rendezvous with her according to Plan B. Anneka smiled as she read the last text. When she had suggested an alternative plan all those months ago, way back in Holland, Gert had laughed and said that it sounded like some James Bond spy movie, but here he was following her instructions and just as well too.

Plan B was that in the event of one or other of them being split up they should find their way to Vancouver. Using false passports and credit cards they would then choose any flight that would put in a substantial distance from Canada. Australia or New Zealand would have been Anneka's prime choice although she wasn't sure where Gert would choose. She texted him and told him that she would meet him according to Plan B and her approximate time of arrival would be determined by when the train left for Toronto and then her connection to Vancouver. She would check with the railway timetable and let him know dates and times later, but right now, she had to walk to the station and then settle in to wait for the train.

AS SOON AS Gert read Anneka's text message, which wasn't until later that night, after he had checked into a dive of a motel just outside of Wawa, he felt such a sense of relief that she was fine that he almost wept as much from relief as from sheer exhaustion. He had been on the road for eighteen hours and, although the motel was a bit of a dump, Gert barely noticed. As soon as his head hit the pillow his eyes closed and he was out like a light.

Anneka, on the other hand, had to wait a couple of hours for a train to Toronto, but was fortunate to catch the first one out in the early hours of the morning, to Vancouver. She was able to sleep once aboard the train and this she finally succumbed to, and like Gert, the minute her eyes were closed, she was dead to the world.

THE ONLY PERSON not to have slept well that night was Karel de Vries. The cell he was locked up in was musty smelling and most certainly not designed for comfort. He was to be deported back to Holland on a KLM flight scheduled for eleven o'clock the following day.

FORTY-NINE

R ose woke up feeling one hundred percent better in every way. It was amazing how a good night's sleep could restore the equilibrium so well. The first thing she did on waking was to phone the hospital. Tom apparently had woken early saying that he was desperate for a cup of tea and was also starving hungry. That made Rose laugh as he was certainly on the road to recovery.

No sooner had she put the phone down, the first of many calls started to come through. Jessica was the first call and she was angry with her mother for not getting back to her. Rose tried to explain that it had been far too late to call when she had finally got in last night and that she had been so exhausted that she had gone straight to bed, but Jessica still bemoaned the fact that she had been so worried and it had been cruel not to have let her know the status of her father. Nothing could placate her daughter so Rose gave up trying.

There were calls from Paul, Anne, Doug, several other friends, and finally one from DCI Hargreaves saying,

"Rose, I just wanted to ask how Tom was doing?"

"Oh, he's doing really well, John. In fact, I'm probably going to bring him home today all providing his blood pressure readings are fine."

"That's great, really great news. I might swing by later this afternoon as I'll be back in Bayfield to wrap up the investigation. I'd like to say my goodbyes."

Rose felt a twinge of sadness creep over her. Somehow John Hargreaves had got under her skin and it saddened her to think that they may not see each other ever again.

"That would be lovely, John, but please feel that you can visit us anytime in Bayfield."

She wanted to cry out that she'd miss him, but it wouldn't have been proper, an old married woman like her.

John too, felt an edge of some emotional feeling which he couldn't explain, an almost sense of despair at the thought of not seeing Rose Blair ever again. How could he be feeling this way over a married woman, no less and one of whom he had only known for one week. He said his goodbye and pulled himself together as he had his team to debrief, The Lion's Hall to clean up, and then The Little Inn to check out of before popping over to The Blairs for one final goodbye.

FIFTY

From Wawa, Gert got an early start and was back on the road again by five-thirty. He would be leaving Ontario behind finally that day and aim to reach Regina by the end of the day. Anneka would, in all likelihood, reach Vancouver before him, but that was alright, he would only be one day behind.

Roaring through the countryside on the Trans Canada Highway, through Manitoba and the flat prairies, Gert was struck at how different the landscape was between the two countries, Holland and Canada. Back home his terrain was polders banked up by dykes and canals. Essentially Holland had been built upon reclaimed land where the early engineers had built a series of ditches or dykes to drain the water, and sand was pumped in to form banks of land. As a consequence, many towns were sinking, including Amsterdam which was estimated at sinking at a rate of 40mm per day.

In contrast in northern Ontario he had felt that he was drowning in trees, everywhere he drove were forests of trees. The old lumberjack song came to his mind and he now understood how Canada had got its reputation as the lumber capital of the world. These days, though, large paper mills lay abandoned, long since deserted and closed down due to wood manufactured cheaply from China. It seemed such a waste of natural resources, Gert thought although the plus side was that chemicals would no longer pollute the rivers and streams of Northern Ontario.

He had seen a moose amble slowly across the highway that morning and the animal appeared to be oblivious to the sound of his motor bike and, indeed, of anything. He had marveled at the size of the beast. Back in Holland there were deer and elk but nothing to match the grand scale of the huge moose. Yes, it was a vast country and the province of Ontario seemed to go on forever.

Gert stopped just outside Winnipeg before entering Saskatchewan and was amazed at the speed and quick timing that he made travelling through the prairies. By ten o'clock that night he had reached his goal, Regina, and had checked into another fleabag motel. His body felt as if it had been tossed through a mangle and his legs wouldn't stop shaking. He was so tired from his journey. Lying in bed he turned the television on and was just in time to watch the CBC news. To Gert's utter amazement, there on the screen was a picture of Karel de Vries with the news flash that said the man had been deported to stand trial in Holland for the murder of Gerrit Van Heuzen.

Gert immediately texted Anneka who had just arrived in Vancouver. She answered him straight away. He had so many questions but was momentarily tongue tied until he finally managed to ask about Karel who he thought was dead. Anneka told him the whole story including being held in custody in London after Karel had tried to strangle her.

Gert then breathed a sigh of relief saying, "I honestly was

finding it difficult to reconcile myself to you as a killer. To be honest I'm so pleased that you didn't succeed as it makes me feel so much better."

They both agreed to meet in front of the Vancouver Public Library in twenty-four hours. In the meantime, Anneka was to find a suitable Airbnb for them to stay in while they decided their future plans. Gert went to sleep that night feeling that a heavy weight had been lifted off his shoulders. Forgery he could deal with, but murder was something else altogether.

FIFTY-ONE

DCI Hargreaves wiped the white board in The Lion's hall clean of all the notes that had been written during the course of the investigation. It barely seemed possible that only one week had passed, it felt like months. In that short time he had experienced a real sense of comradeship with his small team and he sincerely hoped that he would get to work with them all again sometime in the future.

As to the village of Bayfield, well, he had fallen in love with its charm and planned to return, but not in the capacity of a police investigation, instead as a tourist. Rachael and Mike would love it and baby Amelia would so enjoy playing in the sand on the beach. For himself, he hadn't had the luxury of time to have explored the marina and he did so want to go sailing again. He knew that he would return soon and maybe, just maybe, one day he might think about moving to the village himself. For now, he had to wrap up the case by debriefing his team. They had all ambled in, Shopbike coffee in hand, and were looking at him expectantly.

"Good morning everyone. Congratulations on a job well done. Yesterday's arrests went like clockwork and everyone worked well together as a team. Thank you. Now, as to the charges laid I have to say that I am disappointed as I know you all will be. Karel de Vries is being deported back to Holland where he will stand on trial for the murder of Gerrit Van Heuzen. He is already retracting his original statement even though I have it on record. He claims that he was interviewed under duress. Anyhow, it is out of our hands now and as far as I'm concerned, we handled the case with the utmost professionalism.

As to Doctor Moleevaar, I'm afraid to say that she was released last night on the grounds of insufficient evidence. She claimed that the so-called attempted murder of Karel de Vries was nothing more than S&M sex games gone wrong. Our only loose end is Gert Dupuis and the missing painting as both seem to have vanished into thin air. The Commissionaire is reluctant for us to pursue this line of enquiry as The Rijks Museum has not issued any statement about a stolen Vermeer and as far we know, *The Milkmaid* is still hanging on the museum's wall. I have my strong suspicions that Dr. Moleevaar will attempt to lay claim on the Vermeer sooner rather than later, after all, she's already waited twenty years, she won't be giving up too easily. My guess is that she'll be joining up with Gert Dupuis somewhere and what happens then, well we'll have to wait and see. Any questions before I wrap this all up?"

Constable Elliot put his hand up.

"Yes, Constable," DCI Hargreaves said.

"So, Gert Dupuis was the man who painted the forged paintings, sir?"

"Yes, he actually was the most important man in the whole scam although, according to Constable Ryan's notes, he only got put away for ten years. He claimed that all he did was paint reproductions and what happened to them after they were completed was none of his concern. Isn't that correct, Constable Ryan?"

Holly nodded her head and added, "Yes, he always claimed to have known nothing about the selling of the paintings and expressed no interest in that part of the business. He went to school with Karel, Gerrit, and Dr. Moleevaar so it appears that they were all three good friends as much as business partners."

John continued, taking up where Holly had left off, "It appears, but this is only speculation, that Dr. Moleevaar and Gert formed a close relationship after he was released, and they proceeded to scheme and plan to retrieve the stolen Vermeer. It looks as if the doctor deliberately visited, and then formed a close relationship with Karel, in order to have him lead her to the Vermeer. From my interview with Karel it appears that it had been her idea to have Gerrit murdered. It strikes me that Dr. Moleevaar is one scheming, murderous woman."

Sergeant Flowers added, "Yes, well if I was Gert Dupuis, I'd be watching my back. It's pretty obvious that she's just after one thing, and that's the Vermeer."

DCI Hargreaves smiled and continued, "Yes, Sergeant, you're probably right, anyway, it's out of our hands now. We have issued photographs of Gert Dupuis to all detachments, but we have no real cause for arrest. No, we'll just have to file it away, although I'd like to bet that this is not the last time that we'll hear about Dr. Moleevaar. Right, lunch is on me at The Little Inn."

John went ahead of his team to book a table and then to check out of his room. After lunch he would pop around to say his goodbyes to Rose and Tom Blair, although he wasn't sure if either of them would be at home.

The lunch at The Little Inn was exceptionally good and at the end of the meal John proffered a toast to his team and wished them all well. He genuinely felt sad at the thought of disbanding the group. Constable Ryan and Sergeant Flowers worked out of the London office, but Constables Elliot and Brown were from the OPP detachment in Goderich. He certainly would not be seeing them again unless another serious crime came about.

After the team had all dispersed, John settled the bill, walked out to his car and drove around the corner to Bayfield Terrace to the Blair's house. Rose was just getting into her car when John pulled up. She walked over to him and he got out of his car.

"Rose, I'm so glad to have caught you in time. I just wanted to say goodbye and to thank you for everything."

Rose stood there just staring at John and wanting so much to kiss him. Instead she smiled and put out her hand to shake, feeling suddenly rather awkward and unsure of herself.

"I was just about to head over to London to pick Tom up. He's coming home today."

The whole time she had been talking, John had kept hold of her hand. Without saying a single word, he suddenly pulled her to his chest into a tight embrace and then Rose found herself turning her face up to kiss him and feeling herself go weak at the knees as his lips touched hers and they hungrily kissed passionately. *Just what am I doing*, Rose thought, as she pulled away and straightened her dress.

"I'm so sorry," John said, "I really didn't mean to do that, please forgive me."

Rose felt herself blushing and she didn't quite know what to say. "Oh John. I really must be going."

They both stood just looking at each other a while longer and then Rose got back into her car and reluctantly drove off leaving John standing by his car watching her drive away.

Just what was that about, John thought, *what madness came over me,* and he got into his car and headed out back to London pondering his feelings for a married woman called Rose.

FIFTY-TWO

Gert left Regina at five thirty that morning. He had a very long drive ahead aiming to reach Vancouver later that night. He would plan to have lunch in Calgary before heading out over the Rockies and down to the West Coast. It was funny, he mused, how people in Grand Bend referred to Lake Huron and the shores as The West Coast. Thinking about Grand Bend naturally segued into dwelling about Anneka. Gert was having severe doubts about his relationship with the woman. The previous night in the lonely motel room he had pretty well convinced himself that she was only after the Vermeer painting and possibly his skills as an artist able to reproduce paintings. In other words, she was really only in it for the money. Deep down Gert had always known that Anneka had a cold, hard hearted edge to her, but he had foolishly kidded himself that she really loved him and that her black heart had only been aimed at Karel and Gerrit. Now, in the cold light of day, he kicked himself for being so gullible. As he biked across the prairies, he started to formulate an idea, so that by the time he had reached Calgary, Gert had a neat plan just waiting to be put in place.

The scenery had changed from flat, open prairies growing corn and wheat to more fields of crops, but this time with the majestic Rockies rising up in the distance providing an amazing backdrop to the scenery. Calgary itself was built on undulating hills with high rise condo's everywhere. Gert motored to the city centre, pulled into a car park, and took out his phone. Scrolling through the Calgary Business Directory he found the location of the nearest Fed Ex office. Grabbing the artist's canister from the back of his bike, he set off at a brisk pace with purpose; Gert needed to find an art supply shop and then the Fed Ex depot both of which he accomplished within the hour. Arriving at the Fed Ex office carrying not one, but now two artist's canisters, he checked in at the front desk. He had sealed both the tubes with duct tape and the woman at the counter serving him handed over two sticky labels to fill in, which were then stuck on the outside of the canisters.

"So, this one goes to Papeete in Tahiti, correct?" She held up the lighter of the two tubes which actually contained the Vermeer, "And this one is being sent to our office in Victoria, correct?"

The second tube contained art supplies, paint brushes, tubes of paint rolled up in a canvas cloth.

"Okay, that will be forty dollars for the two, sir," she concluded, and Gert handed over his credit card.

"Thank you, Piet, we can guarantee this one will reach Victoria no later than tomorrow, however the tube being sent to Tahiti will probably take at least one week before delivery, is that okay?"

"Certainly, ma'am, that's great. Have a good day."

Gert tucked his collection slips, one in his wallet, and the other more important one, he decided to hide on his motorbike in the small luggage space under the pillion seat. Anneka would never think to look there. Gert had at last put his plan into action.

FIFTY-THREE

Crossing the Rockies was almost a sublimely religious experience for Gert. The beauty of the terrain with the majestic mountains was absolutely breathtaking. There was a sign that said Lake Louise and Banff and much evidence of what would be in the winter, ski resorts. In the distance he could see a small lake which appeared almost turquoise in colour. Everything appeared picture postcard perfect. His poor Honda laboured the ascent over the mountain passes and Gert tried not to look down at the sheer drops to the side of the mountains. He forced himself to concentrate and soon reached the peak and was then roaring down the zigzagged highway getting closer and closer to Vancouver.

There had been dreadful forest fires earlier on in the season and great swaths of land now lay blackened to each side of him. California had been hit the hardest, but British Columbia had received its fair share of the deluge by fire. Before long he could see the sprawling suburbs of Vancouver and in the distance, he could see the Pacific Ocean.

By the time Gert reached the outskirts of the city, it was

already turning dark, he would check into a motel and arrange to meet up with Anneka the next day.

Once again, he found his legs quivering like jelly from fatigue, so much so that he could barely walk to his motel room. His long bike ride was finally over, Tahiti would be the next port of call, with or without Anneka.

Anneka had spent the day shopping in Vancouver. Because she had left London in such a hurry, she had no toiletries, night wear, or even a change of clothing. She had also found a lovely Airbnb right downtown; a small, but beautiful apartment, just perfect for the two of them. The other task Anneka had set herself was to plan how she would rid herself of Gert Dupuis once she had her hands on the Vermeer. She still couldn't believe how foolish she had been to think she could have taken off with the fishing rod case containing the Vermeer that night when she had attempted to kill Karel. In hindsight, Anneka thought, she had tried to be too clever by leaving it there for the police to find and then turning up at The Lion's Hall in her professional capacity as an Art Specialist. What was she thinking? If she had just taken the Vermeer and run, none of this would have been necessary. Now, she had to plan another possible murder and escape, and it was all beginning to get her down.

Quite another issue at hand was the art buyer she had contacted. He was in Las Vegas, not exactly a short distance away. Maybe she could arrange to meet him halfway although, looking at the map Anneka realized that would put her somewhere in Oregon. It was just that Las Vegas was in the middle of nowhere and Nevada appeared to be a vast State. Halfway could mean a meeting place in Portland, Medford, or Eugene.

The Crater Lake National Park covered a large area of central Oregon and that would not be practical arranging to meet in a national park. She would have to fly regardless of where the rendezvous was set and, for forty million dollars, she was prepared to even fly to Las Vegas although she was keen to meet on neutral territory and did not want the art buyer to call all the shots. She would text him and see how compliant he might be in terms of a meeting place. With that decided, Anneka went back to scheming what to do about Gert.

FIFTY-FOUR

Almost two thousand miles away in Ontario, in the sleepy village of Bayfield, nestled on the shores of another completely different west coast, Rose and Tom settled in for the evening. Having picked Tom up from the hospital they had driven back home in almost complete silence. Tom, although feeling so much better, still felt incredibly tired and drained of energy; he was finding it hard to even keep his eyes open on the journey home. Whereas Rose was still feeling riddled with guilt over her uncalled-for kiss with John Hargreaves, and, more to the point, her feelings for the man. It seemed utterly incongruous that after forty years of happy marriage to a man she dearly loved, that in a time of their lives when Tom needed her more than ever, she should find herself attracted to another man.

Fortunately, the minute they had arrived home, Ben and Puff had gone absolutely crazy seeing Tom and then Kate turned up with her new little dog, Lucy who entertained them all with her antics. Lucy should have been a circus dog as she performed perfectly to the delight of all in the room. Sitting with her paws up in the air in a begging position she let out a gentle bark.

Kate laughed and then said, "Roll over, Lucy," and the little dog lay down and rolled over on the floor. "Oh, you're such a clever little dog," Kate crooned. She was clearly besotted with the darling, little fox terrier.

Rose made some tea although she really felt like something much stronger, and she brought the tray out into the sun lounge. The sun was just beginning to set, and Rose and Tom were desperate to go to bed, but Kate was so excited to show her new puppy off that Rose didn't want to burst her bubble.

"So, Rose, I never did get to say goodbye to that handsome detective Hargreaves. What a nice guy. I do hope that we get to see him again. Did you get to say goodbye to him?"

Rose felt her cheeks burn red, she felt like a scarlet woman, what was wrong with her, after all, it was only a kiss. She answered her sister, "I did actually see him briefly. He came back to Bayfield for one last debriefing of the team and then he popped over here just as I was about to drive to London to get Tom."

"Well, I hope he returns one day, I really liked him."

Rose was saved from further discussion by the phone ringing. It was Jessica wanting to talk to her father. Kate took the hint and said that she should go, putting little Lucy on her leash, she went over to Tom to give him a kiss and then Rose, leaving them to walk around the corner to her house.

Anne was next to phone and then Paul, by the time he had finished talking, Tom was ready to go to bed. Rose said that she would take Puff and Ben for a quick walk. She desperately needed some time to herself to process her feelings. Walking down to Pioneer Park she let the dogs off at the top of the stairway leading down to the beach. Standing on the bluff looking out at the magnificent sunset with reds, yellows, and purples layered in strata of cloud reflecting off the vast lake below. Rose could almost loose herself in the sheer aesthetic beauty of the scene before her. Suddenly her phone dinged, and she pulled it out of her pocket and glanced at the screen. Rose let out a small gasp, it was none other than John Hargreaves. She answered the phone straight away.

"Oh, hi John, this is a surprise, how are you?"

There was a pause on the other end of the line and then he answered softly, "Rose, I feel so bad, I should never have kissed you the way I did. It was completely out of character, please forgive me."

"There is nothing to forgive, John. It takes two to tango and I kissed you back." Here she paused before continuing, "and I can't stop thinking about the way I feel too."

Rose heard John let out a deep groan and then he said in a husky voice, "Rose, I don't understand any of this, I really don't, but I haven't felt alive like this in years. Since Mary died, I've been totally celibate. I thought that I would never feel passion or love ever again. Rose, my body yearns for you."

Oh dear, oh dear, Rose thought, what had they done, she would have to put a stop to this before both their feelings got totally out of hand. It was ridiculous as she was a happily married woman and had never been unfaithful to Tom in all their forty years of marriage.

"John, now listen to me. We are both mature adults and we do know that actions have consequences. Much as I'm aware that you and I could have an amazing relationship together, I will not deem to put Tom or any of my family through this. Oh, I know that we could be discreet, plenty of other people have extra-marital affairs, but I wouldn't be able to live with myself or the consequences of my actions if I had to lie to Tom.

So, we're going to nip this in the bud and stop this silliness before it even gets started. I wish you well and please understand that this is very hard for me too."

John answered her quietly. "My dear, Rose, I know that what you are saying is right and proper and I will most certainly respect your wishes, but please say that if you ever change your mind, you will let me know straight away."

"Take care, John. Take care." Rose whispered and ended the phone call.

It was pitch dark now, so she called the dogs, put them on their leashes and proceeded to walk back home deep in thought.

FIFTY-FIVE

Gert woke up after sleeping like a log. Today he would see Anneka and hopefully they would be able to plan a future together unless his suspicions were founded, and she was about to double cross him. It was funny, he thought, how excited he felt at the prospects of seeing his girl again for, despite her obsession with the Vermeer, they both actually enjoyed each other's company and got on well with each other.

The early morning sun rose and shed a pink, hazy light over the city. People appeared to be walking, running, or cycling everywhere and cars lined the roads bumper to bumper along the crazy busy streets of Vancouver. He managed to weave in and out of the cars which appeared to barely be moving. On his motorbike, counting his blessings for his mode of transport.

Gert finally reached the Vancouver Public Library which stood out like a sore thumb in the streetscape of the city. He had texted Anneka before leaving the motel to let her know that he would be at their meeting place by midmorning and looking at the clock on the building he realized it was almost time. Gert looked around anxiously and suddenly he saw her sitting on a bench right in front of the entrance to the library. She was wearing a pair of white shorts, a bright green t-shirt, and her feet clad in strappy sandals. Anneka stood up as soon as she saw Gert and ran towards him waving her arms and hands in a warm greeting. They embraced and then she suggested that they go straight to the Airbnb which was just around the corner from the library. Gert followed Anneka pushing his bike alongside as he walked at her side. They soon came to a small duplex neatly painted white with bright blue shutters on the outside. Gert locked his bike up and left it around the back of the building. Anneka showed him into the apartment, which was perfectly tidy and modern, but very small, although ideal for their own short stay. As soon as they closed the front door, Anneka grabbed Gert and led him into the compact bedroom. The double bed appeared to take up most of the space in the room, but that didn't matter for Anneka and Gert only needed the bed for what they both had in mind. Twenty minutes later they both lay back totally satiated.

Anneka then said, "Okay, Gert, where is it? Where's the painting?"

Oh, oh, here we go, Gert thought, *it hadn't taken her long to cut to the chase.* "Oh, I sent it by Fed Ex to Victoria to the Fed Ex office there, we can pick it up tomorrow."

Anneka frowned and was about to say something and then stopped herself, however a few minutes later she asked Gert, "How will you retrieve the parcel? Do you have to show any I.D. or anything?"

Gert smiled to himself, the lady was truly fishing, but he answered her quickly, "Well, I'll have to show the receipt slip I was given at the Fed Ex office in Calgary when I mailed it, but they didn't say anything about showing any I.D."

Anneka lay in bed thinking. If she could get hold of the shipment slip then she would be able to take the ferry across to Victoria herself, retrieve the painting, and then fly from Victoria to meet up with the art buyer whether it be in Oregon or Nevada. She got out of bed telling Gert that she would make them both some coffee and while she waited for the kettle to boil, she looked around at Gert's clothes now scattered all over the floor. The Fed Ex slip would probably be inside his wallet and that would be in his shorts pocket. Silently she tiptoed over to the bedroom and quickly looked to where Gert lay sprawled totally naked on the bed. He appeared to be sleeping and so she crept in and picked up his shorts. Sure enough, his wallet was tucked in the back pocket of his shorts, she quickly opened it and found the slip tucked in amongst some twenty-dollar bills. Next, Anneka picked up her own clothes, dressed herself quickly, scribbled a quick note saying, *out of cream, be back soon.* She then grabbed her small hold-all which she had packed with her new purchases, and then she slipped out the front door and hailed a taxi.

Gert opened his eyes the minute that he heard the front door click. He was momentarily filled with a sense of loss and sadness as Anneka had taken the bait and a small voice inside of him had really wanted to have proven that his misgivings and intuition were unfounded, but no, she had shown her true colours and now he would stick to his own plan and forget about Anneka. Getting dressed quickly, Gert spent the following hour online booking his air tickets to Tahiti. He then cleaned the little apartment before closing the front door forever. His next move was to sell his motorbike. He had checked online for the nearest Honda dealership and was pleasantly surprised to find one close to the airport. Everything was slotting into place perfectly, just one more piece of the puzzle before he could relax and restart his future.

FIFTY-SIX

Anneka missed the ferry she had hoped to catch and sat waiting in the small coffee shop by the ferry terminal for the next ferry which would take her to Victoria. She, like Gert, had spent some time online sorting out airline tickets and timetables. There was a flight going out of Victoria at four that afternoon by sea plane to Seattle arriving at 4:30. There was a connecting flight to Portland, Oregon at five and from there Anneka would either rent a car and drive to Eugene, where she had proposed to meet the art dealer; or if he had not made contact by the time that she reached Portland, she would take a plane to Las Vegas and meet up with him there. For now, though her main focus was on retrieving the art canister containing the precious Vermeer, from the Fed Ex depot in Victoria.

Gert had no problem selling his motorbike at the dealership and with some of the money he decided to go shopping for new clothes and art supplies which, ironically, he had already purchased a mere twenty-four hours ago. After that he had decided to do a bit of sightseeing as his flight to San Francisco wasn't leaving until later that evening. Stanley Park had featured in most of the tourist information he had read about online. It was within easy walking distance of the city centre too which meant he could walk to it easily. As he approached the park Gert was amazed at the great forest of trees that seemed to emerge out of the green space like sentinels to a fort. Some of the cedar trees looked to be well over one hundred feet tall, almost as tall as some of the high-rise buildings in the city. Foot paths wove in and out of the forest into magic clearings where park benches were placed at intervals. Gert observed a number of homeless people camped out in some of the more secluded forest areas. Back in Europe they would be called gypsies and would be moved on after a few days of encampment. He suspected that the same fate would befall these people, like displaced people throughout the world.

Gert emerged along one side of the park at a viewing point overlooking the bay. He could see a stunning suspension bridge spanning across the Burrard Inlet. He checked online at what he was looking at and found that the iconic bridge was called The Lions Gate and it connected Vancouver city centre with the north shore. It had been officially opened in May 1939 by King George VI and Queen Elizabeth. The bridge was built, or at least funded by the Guinness family for six million dollars and it spanned 473 metres as a single span. The amazing thing was that it had only taken one year to build the structure. Gert stood looking at the magnificent view for some time before returning to the city centre where he took a taxi out to the airport. He would have dinner after he had checked in and then he would try to get a little shut eye before boarding the plane for the first lap of his journey. It was only a relatively short one, three and a half hours to San Francisco and then he had a two hour stop over before a nine hour flight to Papeete in Tahiti. Gert felt tired just thinking about the long journey ahead of him.

FIFTY-SEVEN

Just as he was getting ready to check in at Vancouver Airport, Anneka was being checked in for her short twenty-minute flight from Victoria airport to Seattle. But whereas Gert had a total of twelve and a half hours of travelling time ahead of him, she barely had two hours of which forty minutes was by airplane. She still had not heard from the art dealer in Las Vegas and it might be that she would end up flying to Las Vegas herself if he wasn't going to meet her halfway. In retrospect, she should have just agreed to do just that. As it was, she had been hard pushed for time getting to the airport after being delayed at the Fed Ex office while they searched for the art canister. Anneka hadn't even opened the tube up as Gert had taped it rather too securely with duct tape. She would need a knife to open it and that was not high on her agenda at that moment. She did wonder what Gert was doing back in Vancouver. He would have discovered she was sure, that the Fed Ex slip was missing. How he would react, she wasn't sure as she had never seen the dark side of the man. She knew that he would be sorely hurt by her duplicity. Of the three men, Karel, Gerrit, and Gert, he was by far the most trusting and naïve and she had found that refreshing in a man. Oh well, there were plenty of fish in the sea and with forty million dollars to play with she would have great fun laying the bait to catch one.

FIFTY-EIGHT

Three thousand miles away back in sleepy Bayfield, but three hours later with the time difference, Rose and Tom were preparing to go to bed. Rose had just returned from taking the dogs for a walk and Tom was loading the dishwasher, when the phone rang. It was Susan Parker phoning from Tuscany. Rose looked at the time, it was nine o'clock Ontario time, but it would be twelve by European time. Her heart gave a little jolt as a late call like that could only mean bad news.

"Rose, is that you, Rose?" Susan's voice came through sounding faint and slightly crackly.

"Yes, oh hi, Susan, speak up, the line is dreadful."

"Rose, I'm flying home tomorrow, I just wanted you to be the first to know."

Rose looked and felt alarmed, "But why, Susan, I thought you were staying at least another couple of months. What's happened?"

"Oh, Rose, it's too long a story to tell you over the phone, but I'll tell you everything tomorrow, I promise. Could you go and open up my house and maybe get in some groceries like milk, coffee and bread, yes, and lots of coffee. Now ciao, ciao. I'll see you tomorrow."

Before Rose could say anything else, Susan had cut the line leaving her holding the phone with a perplexed look on her face.

"What was all that about, love?" Tom asked.

"Oh, Tom, that was Susan phoning from Italy. Something is dreadfully wrong. She's coming home tomorrow, and she hasn't told me why."

Tom was pensive for a while and then he said, "It sounds as if things haven't gone well with her relationship with Tonne. Don't worry, love. She'll be all right and it may not be as bad as you think."

But it is, Rose thought, she just knew that what Susan Parker had to tell her would not be good news and her heart sank for her dear friend.

FIFTY-NINE

The plane landed exactly on time at Portland Airport in North Oregon State. As soon as the passengers had disembarked Anneka turned on her cell phone and there, to her express relief, was a message from the art buyer from Las Vegas. Due to business constraints, he could not get away, but would happily meet her at his hotel in Vegas the following day. Anneka paused before answering him, she had hoped to have met him on neutral territory, but the hotel lobby or lounge would have to do. She texted him back asking what time would work for him. In the meantime, she would check into a hotel in Portland and get some well-deserved sleep. Tomorrow would be another day and she would face it much better after a good night's sleep.

Sleep was what Gert craved more than anything as he finally boarded the plane that would take him on the final leg of his journey to Tahiti. The two hour stopover in San Francisco had been grueling just trying to stay awake, drinking cup after cup of strong Starbucks Coffee, so that when he finally could crash, he was just far too wired up to let sleep come, and then, just as he felt heavy eyed, the flight attendant came around offering drinks and snacks. Gert groaned as he pulled up the light blanket and snuggled up to the small pillow that he had found on his seat. He was determined to sleep come what may, he needed to be fresh and alert for his arrival in nine hours time.

Gert had spent much time planning what he would do when he arrived in Papeete. The first thing was to find some accommodation and then he could set up his studio. The next thing he needed to do was to purchase some canvases stretched and prepped for him to very specific measurements, and then probably the most challenging of all the items on his list, was acquiring the right stones and pigments to grind to make his very special paints. He might have to order those online, he had already sussed out a supplier of azurite from Australia and he could probably get all his rocks from the same source if he was unable to find a local supplier. He had researched potential houses to rent on MLS and there were no shortages. He also found a number on Airbnb and Vrbo. It was positively amazing what could be done online, it had made his life that much easier. The last item on his planning list was finding a potential buyer for the Vermeer painting. Unbeknownst to Anneka, Gert had been conducting his own research into art collectors and had found several buyers of fine art living right in the Polynesian Islands. He would start up a dialogue with them when he had got himself settled. With that last point clarified in his mind, Gert closed his eyes and finally slept the sleep of the dead, so much so that he didn't wake up again until the plane was in its final descent. He was almost at his destination and final goal post.

SIXTY

The last text message from the Las Vegas art buyer actually ended with his full name, Lioness Hoffe-meyer. In the previous text messages, he had just signed off with LH, so that now knowing his full name, Anneka had something to go on. Googling Lioness Hoffemeyer she was startled to find that he owned what looked like half of Las Vegas's real estate. At least five hotels and casinos not to mention shopping malls; the man was a billionaire. She studied the picture of him which accompanied the Google search. He looked a very hard man, very Jewish and with a name like Hoffemeyer she was not in the least bit surprised. According to the search he was a man in his fifties with three marriages under his belt and four children. His art collection was world renowned with mostly renaissance paintings, although he had just started collecting the Old Dutch Masters and now owned several Rembrandts and Vermeer's. He sounded an interesting man and in a different life she might have liked to have got to know him better. For the time being, though, Anneka needed to get some sleep as the following day would, she was sure, be very busy.

SHE AWOKE the next day to a beautiful morning. The sky was a clear blue with not a single cloud to be seen, a far cry from the rain she had left behind in both Victoria and Seattle. With the bright weather, her spirits lifted. She had arrived at the airport a good half hour before her flight, in fact, just as Gert's plane was then landing in Tahiti, although neither were aware of the other's plans.

Portland to Las Vegas was an hour's plane ride away. Anneka arrived at her hotel by ten that morning. She was meeting Lioness Hoffemeyer at eleven thirty in the hotel lobby which she had already observed on her arrival. Anneka decided to dress herself in one of her new purchases and to make herself up so that she would make a good first impression. Suddenly a little bubble of excitement rose up in her throat, all of the years of planning were finally coming into fruition.

SIXTY-ONE

S usan Parker flew into Pearson in Toronto from the Galileo Airport in Pisa, Tuscany. She had taken the ferry across from Porto Ferrari on the island of Elba where Tonne and she had rented a villa. Every time she thought about Tonne her heart missed a beat, how could she have been so terribly wrong about the man when usually her instincts were normally on the mark, but not this time, she had most certainly got it all wrong.

Oh, the first month of their honeymoon, living on the idyllic island of Elba was wonderful. Tonne had been attentive to her every need, they had lived in a state of euphoria, eating when they felt like it, swimming in the azure waters of the Mediterranean, drinking loads of Italian wine, and making love whenever the mood took them.

Everything was going like a dream until they met Luigi Delfortino, the businessman from Rome. When Susan looked back, she could pinpoint the very time and the place where it had all begun, the beginning of the end so to speak of everything.

Luigi owned a yacht that was anchored in the harbour at Porto Ferrari. Tonne had met him one morning when he was out running, and they had instantly become friends. They had been invited to a few parties on the boat and Susan soon realized that they were out of their depth. The party revelers were all part of the jet set, mostly from Rome, mostly wealthy and all of them into snorting cocaine. It was there that it all began, the furtive looks, the excuses and lies, the dripping nose, and the mood swings. At first Susan had not clued in, although being a retired detective should have given her an edge, but it all came out one evening over a month after meeting Luigi. Tonne had gone out for his morning run on the beach while Susan caught up with laundry and housework. She had prepared lunch on the terrace and had started to worry when Tonne had not appeared by two that afternoon. By three Susan had jumped in their car and was driving around looking for him. She decided to go and ask Luigi for his help and was just pulling into the harbour car park when Tonne appeared, arm in arm with Luigi. It was apparent that both men were high as kites and Susan could barely contain her anger. As soon as she had Tonne in the car she let loose, shouting at him all the way to the villa. It wouldn't have been so bad if Tonne had shown some remorse, but instead, a few days later, he repeated the same behaviour and so it went on.

The most depressing part for Susan was that he showed no feelings for his actions. Susan could hardly wait for Luigi and his friends to leave the island, but unfortunately, he had moored his yacht for the summer. Tonne appeared to be having the time of his life snorting cocaine with the rich and famous; something had to give. The straw that broke the camels back was when Susan found that all the money in her purse had been taken. Money that had been set aside to pay for groceries and the rent. Tonne had helped himself to it to pay his debts to Luigi. It transpired that he owed a ton of money, not only to Luigi, but to several other people on the island. Even then Tonne showed little remorse until the day that Susan was paid a visit by a huge gorilla of a man who threatened her in no uncertain terms, that unless Tonne paid the money that he owed him by the end of the week, he would come back and ruin her pretty face. When Tonne heard this, he had blanched and looked guilty and then had broken down and cried like a baby. By the time he had managed to pull himself together enough to tell Susan everything, including how much money he owed, it came out in one big gush.

In the end, Tonne grew very serious and told Susan that he knew how ruthless the men could be, after all, he had been an undercover cop for the drug squad for many years and had met many shady drug dealers in that time. Tonne had been insistent that Susan return to Canada and leave him to sort out the mess that he had created. Susan knew, she just knew that this time he was deadly serious and that worried her more than anything else. The night before she flew back home, they had made deep, passionate love and Tonne had promised to make amends and to get back to her just as soon as he could. Susan, for once, believed him.

Here she was now driving back to her safe sanctuary in the village of Bayfield and to her friends, Rose and Tom Blair.

SIXTY-TWO

Anneka waited in the lobby of The Hoffemeyer Hotel
pacing up and down and wondering if Lioness
would show up. She held the artist canister in one
hand, still sealed with the duct tape, and she was about to give
up waiting and return the canister to her room when a man
who had to have been Lioness Hoffemeyer, walked into the
hotel with such authority that he almost wanted to make
Anneka stand up straight and salute him. Accompanying the
man were two beefy bodyguards who flanked each side. All
three men wore suits which made Anneka smile as they looked
so formal in their attire and with temperatures outside over
one hundred degrees, she couldn't imagine how hot they
must be.

Lioness stood in the middle of the lobby looking around
him truly like a lion surveying its prey before it pounced.
Anneka had a distinct advantage as she already knew who he
was and so she took the initiative to walk over and introduce
herself to him and suggested that they take a seat in the lounge
area. After the first awkwardness and formality of introducing

themselves, they began to chat easily and Anneka found herself quite liking the man. They talked about his art collection and he, in turn, asked her about the Vermeer. She decided to come clean and tell him the truth about how she had acquired the painting, suspecting that he would respect her more for being honest than if she had spun some other tale.

Finally, he came to the crunch by saying, "So, Anneka, let me see what you have to sell?"

Anneka looked around the busy lounge and then suggested that they maybe go back to his office as revealing the picture in such a public place may not be too sensible saying, "I could follow you back to your office and if you like it, then we could conclude the bill of sale there and then."

Lioness agreed and then suggested that they maybe have lunch together afterwards to celebrate, to which Anneka agreed asking how far away his office was. Lioness replied that it wasn't far at all, but he had his limo waiting outside. He would take her to his office, conclude the business, go out for lunch, and then have her driven back to the hotel afterwards. Anneka smiled, here was a man of action, he cut to the chase and she really liked that in a man.

"Okay, let's do it," she said and picked up her purse and art canister and stood up.

Lioness nodded to his security guards and they all four headed out through the hotels main entrance. A blast of heat hit them, but Anneka didn't mind, she would soon be the owner of forty million dollars, what did a bit of heat matter. The stretched limo was waiting parked directly in front of the hotel. Cars zoomed past along the busy street and as Anneka took in the sights, all the dazzling buildings looked more like a giant movie set than a downtown streetscape.

The security guards had reached the limo and had just

opened the passenger door for Lioness who had waited gallantly by the car side for Anneka whilst looking nervously around. Suddenly, without warning, a loud crack pierced the air and Anneka stood there riveted to the ground just wondering what it was.

Then, as if in slow motion, Lioness crumpled to the sidewalk and the bodyguards started shouting to Anneka, "Get down, get down," and still Anneka just stood there as if she was glued to the ground not really comprehending what had just happened, and then another crack and she felt her body spin around. Her eyes took in the blue, blue of the sky, her hands let go of the precious art canister, her body began to fall, fall, fall, and then there was nothing.

SIXTY-THREE

Susan went around to Rose and Tom's house an hour after she had arrived at her condo on Harbour Court, in Bayfield. She loved her house and even though living in Italy and soaking up the Mediterranean sunshine had been subliminal, there truly was no place like home. She didn't feel quite so desperate now that she was removed from the situation. Living with Tonne and his drug problem over the past two months had felt toxic and she had begun to feel the effects of the poison colouring her everyday life. Now, however, back in her lovely home, she was able to put everything into perspective and things did not appear quite so dire. She had phoned Tonne the minute that the plane had landed and had assured him that she was just fine. They had arranged for the bank to transfer money from Susan's account, enough to pay all of his debts, and Tonne was to settle up with everyone as soon as he could. He had promised to go into rehab when he returned to Canada, and Susan knew of just the place for him near Toronto. After that, and only then, would she allow him back into her life. He would be safe in Bayfield if he kept away from any of his old haunts in London.

The two-hour drive from Pearson Airport to Bayfield had gone by very quickly and Susan had speculated on how green everything was and how, compared to the dusty dryness of the Mediterranean summer, Ontario seemed so positively humid. Arriving in Bayfield she had taken a little detour down the village Main Street and marveled at the number of tourists shopping, although the village still had not lost its charm. Susan eventually got to Harbour Court and her lovely condo and had carried her suitcase into the kitchen and put the kettle on for coffee. Then she had let out a deep sigh, it was so good to be home.

An hour later she was knocking on Rose and Tom's door with a bottle of Italian Chianti wine and the day's Globe and Mail, which had been given out in the plane, in her hands. Susan thought that Tom might appreciate reading the paper.

Rose opened the door and cried out excitedly, "Oh, Susan, you look absolutely fantastic, that suntan you've got and your hair. Come in, come in, oh, I've missed you so much."

Susan came into the house just as Tom walked in through the back door with Puff and Ben in tow.

"Susan, how lovely to see you," he walked over and embraced her.

She pulled away from him and looked at him searchingly, "Tom, are you alright? You've lost so much weight, are you okay?"

Rose said quietly, "Susan, Tom had a heart attack, but he's doing fine, aren't you darling?"

"Yes, everything's fine, I'm just a bit tired."

Susan's face creased with worry as she examined Tom's

face once more. They had always had good chemistry together, in fact, if he hadn't been married to her good friend Rose, Susan just knew that they would easily have become lovers. She shook her head and said quickly, "I've got lots to tell you."

Rose nodded and said, "Yes, you got me really worried last night. Now, I'll go and pour us a nice glass of wine and you can tell us all about your life in Tuscany."

Susan was about to go into the living room when she remembered the newspaper.

"Oh, by the way, Tom, I've got today's paper for you, they were handing them out on the plane."

Tom took the paper and put it on the kitchen counter saying, "Thanks, Susan, now Rose, I'll deal with the wine and leave you two to catch up on everything."

One hour later, Susan and Rose appeared in the kitchen to find Tom sitting at the table reading the paper. Suddenly he shouted out loud, "Good God, Rose, wasn't that woman you had the run in with called Moleevaar, Dr. Moleevaar?"

Rose looked at Tom blankly and then answered, "You mean, Anneka, that nasty, aggressive woman who smashed into my Volvo and didn't even stop. Is that who you mean?"

Susan looked at the two of them with surprise written all over her face, "What's been going on here in my absence?"

Rose ignored her friend and homed in on Tom, "What's this got to do with that woman, Tom?"

Tom read out aloud from The Globe and Mail,

In a bizarre incident involving a world renown Dutch art specialist, Dr. Moleevaar, two people were shot dead in a drive-by shooting. Mr. Hoffemeyer, owner of the Hoffemeyer chain of hotels and casinos, was killed alongside the Dutch national, D.r Moleevaar. Both were experts in the field of art.

Police are investigating other similar gang land related shootings in the city.

"What a way to go," Tom said as he folded the newspaper and prepared to join Susan and Rose on the patio outside.

SIXTY-FOUR

The coconut palms gently swayed in the South Seas breeze. White, white sand stretched as far as his eyes could see with sea so shockingly blue it took your breath away while white crested waves rolled to shore in a steady rhythm.

Gert sat on his balcony taking in the glorious vista before him not quite believing his luck as the view was like something out of a travel brochure. Tahiti had more than surpassed all his expectations as it was just so breathtakingly beautiful. Even his own back yard exuded beauty with the frangipani trees, bougainvillea bushes, and hibiscus flowers everywhere framing his handsome house with an abundance of colour.

As he sketched the view before him on a canvas balanced rather precariously on his knees, he thought about the article that he had just read in The Globe and Mail. It had to have been Anneka, his scheming lover, who else could it have been? The newspaper was three weeks old; he had found it left on a table in his favourite café, Café Germain, on Rue Mon Palais where it had been discarded by the previous reader. Newspapers generally took at least a week to reach Tahiti, often longer, and English papers were rare to find. When Gert stumbled across a copy of the Globe and Mail, he took it greedily wanting to catch up on the news. He never came across Dutch newspapers.

In the three weeks that he had been living in Papeete, Gert had achieved a phenomenal amount, so much so that his original planning list was down to just a few items the biggest of which was the sale of the Vermeer. He got up and walked from his balcony into the living room where hanging on the wall right in the centre of the room, was the magnificent painting, and there, resting on an easel was an almost complete replica of the same picture. Two other easels were set up with blank canvases waiting to be rendered with the same magic brush strokes. Gert smiled and left the room to go for a walk down to the beach.

He had just set off when he noticed a sudden unnatural silence fill the air. Not a sound could be heard, and before his very eyes he watched as the water receded from the beach leaving the fishing boats stranded like beached whales and fish flopping on the wet sand before him.

A SNEAK PEEK AT MURDER AT BAYFIELD RIVER!

Ryan stood at the edge of the approach to the new bridge over the Bayfield River surveying the scene before him. The temporary bypass bridge was in and opened, the old bridge had been demolished and the beginnings of the two large concrete abutments were rising up majestically from each side of the river, bearing the heavy cages of reinforced metal bars which seemed to poke incongruously out of the top of the shutters. The new bridge was beginning to take shape. After months of waiting for the contract to be awarded Ryan was pleased that they were now on schedule and making rapid progress on the planned two-year project.

He looked at his watch. It was only seven o'clock, his best time of the day. The rest of the construction team would be arriving soon, but Ryan always made it a point of arriving half an hour earlier. He liked to start his day peacefully, to enjoy his cup of coffee that he had picked up from Shop Bike on the main street in the village, to light up a cigarette, the one and only of the day, and to give himself time to reflect on the world and the day ahead.

Ryan walked over to the metal safety fence which also overlooked the river flats. There wasn't a single fisherman out on the river that morning, which was quite unusual, until he remembered that there had been a fishing derby just the previous weekend and those same fishermen were probably now enjoying a break from catching fish.

Ryan looked down to where the river meandered and flowed over white rocks and around what looked like an island which spawned tall grasses and a few spindly trees. He could see a deeper channel of water barely twenty feet across where he supposed one could navigate a small boat.

The river looked particularly fresh and sparkling that day with the early morning sun already casting bright rays across the twinkling water. Ryan surveyed the riverbank and then looked back again at what appeared to be a pile of clothing, or maybe some garbage, stuck in the long grasses by the side of the riverbank and close to the actual bridge construction. He glanced at his watch again. There was still fifteen minutes left of his precious peace, time enough to go and investigate the mound of clothing or whatever it was that had caught his attention from above.

Ryan walked back up the hill until he came to the entrance to the river flats. This piece of land, so he had been told, had been purchased by the community and put into trust to be used by the public and to be maintained as natural habitat. There was a small car park at the bottom of the steep hill by the edge of the embankment where the new bridge abutments were taking shape. Ryan walked to the river's edge and looked along the bank trying to find what he had spied from above. Scanning the bank, he suddenly noticed the change in the ebb and flow of the water. He walked towards the unnatural flow and peered down through the tangled mass of reeds and branches. There, barely visible to the naked eye, he could see a leg twisted around a floating log. His eyes followed the limb and realization clicked in that he was looking at the body of a man half submerged in the swirling water channelling around the body like the ebbing tide of a seaside beach.

Ryan pulled out his phone, and feeling strangely detached from the situation, tapped in 911. Later, when asked, he would say that it had all seemed unreal to him finding the body of a man trapped amongst the flotsam of the Bayfield River, and that he had no recollection of even making the phone call to the police. When further asked how he knew that the man was actually dead, Ryan could only say that he just knew without turning the body over, that there was absolutely no life left in the poor soul and that it was pretty obvious that the back of the man's head had been bashed to a pulp.

Murder at Bayfield Beach

Murder at the Croquet Club

Murder at Town Hall

Murder at the Marina

Murder at the Little Inn

Murder at the Retreat

Murder at Windmill Lake

Murder at Bayfield River

Murder at the Mine

ACKNOWLEDGMENTS

There are, as usual, many people to acknowledge in the writing of this, my seventh Rose Blair Murder Mystery novel.

I would like to thank Jennifer Pate and her lovely family for kindly allowing me to begin this novel at their beautiful property set just north of Bayfield in Huron County. If you ever get the chance, call in to see their wonderful Eco Park and spend some time visiting with them.

There are many wonderful people in my life who have listened to me talking about the unfolding plot, murder, and motive for so long that I must apologize for boring the socks off all of you. Thank you for your patience and understanding. I would also like to thank Alison and Paulette for reading the manuscript and providing their comments.

My darling husband has also had to put up with my preoccupation whilst writing and my general reluctance to do any cooking or indeed housework during this intense month of writing. I love you for always being there for me.

Finally, I would like to thank NaNoWriMo the online

writing support group for budding authors, for providing the incentive to get fifty thousand words written in one month. It really has been an endeavour but is also an excellent way to keep me on track.

ABOUT THE AUTHOR

Over the past thirty years Judy has written twenty novellas, various collections of poetry and a number of plays. Judy wrote her first full length novel in 2013 and developed it into a series called the Rose Blair Murder Mysteries all set in the sleepy village of Bayfield on the beautiful shores of Lake Huron in Ontario, Canada.

Judy and her husband reside in Bayfield with their beloved dog Susie and cat Thomas and enjoy visits from their children and grandchildren.

After retiring Judy and her husband took on a new challenge in their lives. Purchasing land on the outskirts of Bayfield they have planted a six acre vineyard and are in the process of designing and building a boutique winery.

Life is beautiful and sweet. I feel so very blessed with all my wonderful family and friends who continually surround me with their love.

FIND OUT MORE!

Find Cozy House Press online to read more great cozy mysteries!

www.cozyhousepress.com

COZY HOUSE PRESS
MAKE A DATE WITH MURDER

www.ingramcontent.com/pod-product-compliance
Lightning Source LLC
Chambersburg PA
CBHW020834260626
47169CB00003B/982